The Sacred Sphere

By G. H. Teed

*First Published in the Christmas Special Number,
Union Jack 2, No. 529, November 29th, 1913.*

Illustrated by Val Reading and Arthur Jones.

Stillwoods Edition, 2019.

Stillwoods.Blogspot.Ca

Catalogue Information:
Title: The Sacred Sphere (illustrated)
Author: G. H. (Hamilton) Teed, (1886-1938)
First published: Christmas Special Number, *Union Jack 2*, No. 529, November 29th, 1913.
Illustrated by: Val Reading and Arthur Jones.
This Edition by: Stillwoods, 2019.
ISBN Canada: 978-1-988304-62-5
Blog: Stillwoods.Blogspot.Ca
Author Blog: GHTeed.Blogspot.Com
Bookstore: http://www.lulu.com/spotlight/lulubook22

A Magnificent 80,000-word Romance!
Written by the author of "The Yellow Sphinx"
A Christmas Story with a Deeply Laid Plot
Introducing Sexton Blake, Tinker, Pedro, Yvonne; Dr. Huxton Rymer, and Wu Ling, Chief of the Brotherhood of the Yellow Beetle.

G.H. Teed, Canada and his prolific writing.

Author G. Hamilton Teed, (1886-1939) New Brunswick, Canada

According to the first census of New Brunswick in 1902, George Heber Teed was born in Benson, New Brunswick, December 1886[1], no date is associated with the birth! He did not like the name Heber and adopted Hamilton[2] as his familiar name. He died 24 December 1938.

He remained in New Brunswick in his formative years, eventually studying at McGill University, Montreal. After that he started to travel the world.

1912 he arrived in London and started a career as a novelist writer of thriller stories which were immensely popular with the urban crowd that was eager for the modern media of paperback periodicals. He wrote suspense and thriller stories that often involved travels to exotic and remote areas of the world. *Twixt Fire and Redskin* appears to be the first appearing in Boys' Friend, issue 597 (16 November 1912). *The Kidnapped Ambassador* in Boys' Friend (30 November 1912) was his second published story.[3]

Steve Holland also relates a few other works otherwise missing from fictionmags:

'Boys of the Bush,' in Cheer Boys Cheer, issue 29, December 7, 1912.

Boys' Friend Library, *'The Great Mining Swindle'* (1913) (1/228)

The Yellow Sphinx, UNION JACK • New series • Issue 512 • 2/8/1913

When Greek Meets Greek (1913), the second Yvonne story. [then Hodder says THE PENNY PICTORIAL · Issue 715 · 8/2/1913 and anon]

"straight science fiction yarns (two appeared in Red Magazine in 1915"

Poisoned Blossoms, Union Jack 2/1305, 20 October 1928 is highly rated. [Hodder does not think it great!]

Dixon Hawke Library [#327, n.d. (11 Jun 1932)] (4d, 132pp)

---

[1] Census of 1901 is available at ancestors.com
[2] ditto
[3] Based upon Steve Holland's *Forgotten Authors Volume 3*. [highly recommended]

The Terror from Devil's Island [Dixon Hawke] · <u>Anon</u>. · n. "…At least five stories…"

"also writing stories and serials for Boys' Journal, Red Magazine, Boys' Realm and Answers Library."[4]

Although he is forgotten today, Teed was one of the foremost writers of his day, and his subject matter—the fictional detectives, Sexton Blake and Nelson Lee. These two were champions of rival publishers in London—publishing new stories every week or so and available on newsstands—and from North American view rivals of Sherlock Holmes.

Teed never forgot New Brunswick or Canada. Some of his highest most recommended reading features New Brunswick and Canada, in order by date:

The Sacred Sphere Union Jack 1913 includes New Brunswick and the Passamaquoddy area, with extensive descriptions. This is a book length story and can be found on Lulu.Com. Mark Hodder says "Simply one of the best Sexton Blake tales of all time."

Bribery and Corruption SB1915. New Brunswick. This novel features a community not unlike Woodstock, NB and the storyline is very commercial in its aspect. A great story with lots of plot twists. Due to its length it will become a paperback reproduction. Hodder rates this as 'Teed at his best!' found on Lulu.

Blue Diamonds NL1916. Labrador, Canada. Blog

The Man Hunters NL1917. Yukon, Canada. Blog

The Mystery in the Big Woods SB1922. New Brunswick. Found on Lulu.

They Shall Repay, UJ2 1930. Sexton Blake features introduction of recurring villain/heroine Mlle. Roxane Harfield, who is the daughter of a New Brunswick forest entrepreneur. Blakiana site's expert, Mark Hodder, rates at 5☆. Tobique and Plaster Rock are mentioned. Found on Blog.

The Crook of Canada, THE SEXTON BLAKE LIBRARY · 2nd series · Issue 236 · Apr. 1930. Contents unknown!

All of these are digitally captured and converted, excepting the last!

---

[4] ditto

★ Summary:

Teed published 48 stories in Detective Weekly from 'philsp'

367 Sexton Blake stories from 'blakiana'; philsp does not seem to have collected Union Jack data. Blakiana is an excellent resource, authored by Mark Hodder.

30 Nelson Lee stories says 'friardale' which attaches PDF when available.

3 stories feature hero, Prof. Sampson Parr says philsp; Holland says these first appeared in Red Magazine.

5 stories feature hero, Cort Jurgens says fictionmags

5 stories feature hero, Black Abbot says fictionmags

3 feature hero, Shadow Crook in Detective Weekly.

2 misc adventure, incl. Caribbean story, **Terror of the Reef**, ss, reproduced in the blog.

In summary it appears Teed wrote **at least 414 stories**! A few of these appear in the GHTeed.blogspot.com site; longer or stories with lots of pictures are converted to books available at Lulu.Com. These are not perfect— I want to read these stories, not to perfect them! Fictionmags site describes the lengths of the stories so I have endeavoured to collect the word count with each story.

Sexton Blake brings his wonderful brain into play, probing and delving for an explanation of Lady Sybil's disappearance.

THE great Dominion of Canada was flinching under the lash of the blizzard. From east to west, from north to south, all the fiercest elements of December seemed to have combined to bury the face of the land beneath a weighty coat of white, and hide beneath towering drifts the roads and trails of plain and valley. For twenty-four hours it had been snowing—not the soft white flakes which fall against the face in delicate caress, but the blinding, cutting, sandy ice-flakes of the blizzard.

In the cities everything was dislocated; in the country travel was impossible. From Halifax to Winnipeg the railway service was in disorder. News filtered through slowly, for most of the telegraph wires were down. Meagre reports arrived, however, of trains being blocked by mountainous drifts through which even the rotary snow-ploughs failed to eat their way. In Nova Scotia a train had been half buried under an avalanche of snow; in Quebec another train had left the rails, and had gone rolling and tumbling into a snowy abyss, to be lost to sight in a deep drift.

But nowhere in that great expanse of country was the blast more fierce, or the drifts more mountainous, than in New Brunswick.

In summer, a green emerald is set in Canada's fair brow; in winter she is a cold white diamond—her great forests bent under the white blanket—her streams and rivers smooth paths of ice—her coasts desolate grey bulwarks against the winter's blast.

Three feet of snow already carpeted her forests before the present storm broke—three feet of white, softness which had come with December.

Then, all had been bustle in her great lumber camps. Gangs of men who had gone in at the approach of winter had been kept busy making the "tote road" along which the huge sleds of logs would go tearing to the river. Other gangs made the woods ring with the steady whirr of the axe in the frosty air.

From dawn to dark, horses and men toiled in the shelter of the woods, the steaming sides of the horses changing to white frost as the cold air condensed against their flanks; and the beards of the men became white fringes of icicles. The breaking of the blizzard had stopped all this, however, and now men and horses were under cover, the former whiling away the time by rough horse-play in the bunkhouse, the latter contentedly munching oats in the rude but warm stables. For it was Christmas Eve and, storm or no storm, the morrow meant a free day.

Still the tempest showed no signs of abating. Even the great herds of moose and caribou and deer sought the retreat of the denser timber; the partridges whirred silently onward to seek the shelter of the wide spreading fir and spruce; the otter and the mink dived deep into the cold but untroubled waters and even the white furred rabbits disappeared into the deepest part of their runs.

King Blizzard reigned supreme.

A PERILOUS DASH THROUGH THE STORM-SWEPT NIGHT

For an hour Looey Sing sat rigid, his eyes peering ahead, his whole attitude one of disregard for storm and ice and darkness until, dead ahead, a single light appeared. Then he bent forward and shut off the engine. (*Page 1.*)

In the far south-west corner of New Brunswick, where that British province breaks into the State of Maine, lies the town of St. Stephen, noted somewhat widely for the past glories of great timber industries, and its present advancing manufactures.

Between it and the American side runs the far-famed St. Croix, that deep blue river which De Monts sailed up over three hundred years ago. Then the high fertile hills which smile down upon it were

3

covered by dense forests of timber, and the Indian was lord.

Now the white man holds it in his sway; the timber has disappeared; the hills have been changed to waving stretches of green; the red man has gone into the Great Unknown, and the habitations of civilisation edge its banks.

But one thing remains unchanged. Its great tides still rise and fall as they flow into or out of Passamaquoddy Bay with the same unbroken regularity which marked them in the time of De Monts and Champlain; of Columbus and Balboa; of the still earlier Norsemen; yea, of the dim unwritten past, before even the red man himself came from the distant shores of Asia.

From the water's edge to the distant height, where the hills became lost in the stormy sky, was all the land under white, for here, too, the blizzard had struck.

Far up the river, where the fresh water predominated, the wharves of the sister towns of the American Calais and the British St. Stephen were locked in ice; but far down, where its the little island of St. Croix, where De Monts landed and where the salt spew of the bay defies the cold, the water was open, only a few rushing cakes of ice, like miniature Arctic floes, telling the conditions which prevailed higher up.

And the swift closing day of the blizzard was Christmas Eve here as everywhere else.

About two miles out of St. Stephen, on the road which leads to the timbered point which guards the entrance to Oak Bay, stands a dilapidated frame building which one might imagine deserted, did it not bear on its front in rude letters "Looey-Sing, Laundry and General Store."

Why a Chinese laundry should be established in such a desolate spot is a matter of mystery. One thing, however, was certain. The word in front was the only evidence there was of a laundry, for none came to Looey Sing with garments to be washed.

It made some pretence of being a general store, for on the shelves were a few rusty tins of vegetables and boxes of tea; a barrel of biscuits formed a convenient nesting-place for the mice which swarmed there; a cask, which was supposed to contain molasses, lay on its side against the wall, and another— presumably oil—butted against it.

A box of onions, a maggotty cheese, a few paper bags, and a

show-case filled with a varied assortment of "candy" mouth organs, chewing gum, and ten cent watch chains, made up the balance of Looey Sing's stock.

At maximum inventory it might go to fifty dollars; at a bankrupt auction it would do well to bring five.

No customers had broken the musty silence of Looey Sing's shop that stormy day. As a matter of fact, the door had not even been unlocked since the preceding afternoon. The lack of custom seemed not to worry the Chinaman, however, for he sat hunched over the little stove in the back room which formed his abode, smoking yellow cigarettes, and gazing with imperturbable calm into the red coals.

From the small square of glass in the rear of the room could be seen a wild snow-covered stretch of woods running down to the river; then the ice-covered bosom of the river itself, clear and blackly sinister, where the howling blizzard whipped the snowflakes from the smooth surface and sent them whirling inwards to the bank; then came the American side of the river, now lost to view in the careering curtain of the storm.

Farther to the left, the unbroken expanse of ice reached its climax, and patches of open water, in which rode small floes, showed where Jack Frost lost his sway. In front of the shack was a rough, little travelled road, now hidden under the drifts, though here and there, where the wind found a spot unprotected, it swept it bare to the frozen mud. No houses could be seen, although several farms surrounded the abode of Looey Sing.

Not until the fading light of early afternoon made it impossible to see did the motionless Chinaman rouse himself from his position. He did so with a slow, cautious movement, and his slant-set eyes darted about as though the lonely spot were the centre of spies interested in his doings—an unconscious habit assumed by Looey

Sing during a long life of curious dealings, and had anyone been interested in the psychological wonder of a laundry in such a place, he might have found in the Celestial's manner a clue to the mystery.

He moved about with Oriental calm and noiselessness. His immediate object was harmless enough, consisting of the preparation of a cup of tea, which he drank after the fashion of the natives of the Shantung hinterland—thick and black. This done, he tidied up again in a scrupulous manner, and approached the pane of glass at the rear.

For some minutes he gazed out at the now invisible river, but the sharp staccato sound of the hail and snow on the window told him the storm still raged.

After a few minutes he turned back, muttering cryptically in pidgin English:

"Twenty mo' at two hunled dollals. Fo' tousand dollars fo' Looey Sing."

Then he replenished the fire and resumed his seat, once more attacking the yellow cigarettes. Not until it was past six did he move.

It was as dark now as it would be at midnight, and neither man nor beast was abroad in that lonely spot, though, in the town further up, a few intrepid spirits had braved the elements, determined to finish their Christmas shopping.

From a cupboard in the corner Looey Sing took out a long coonskin coat and cap of similar fur. When he had donned the coat and had drawn the cap well down on his head, his deep, yellowish eyes peeped out with all the cunning of the little beast from which the fur originally came.

After that he did a surprising thing. He went into the front shop and dropped a bar over the door; that finished, he returned to the rear room and unlocked a door which led out to the back of the shack. It seemed strange that any man should have business outside on such a night, but undoubtedly Looey Sing had.

Throwing open the door, he braced himself and clung to it, for the blast which swept in threatened to tear it from his grasp. With a last glance around the room, he took a long breath and, bending low, stepped out, closing the door after him.

For a moment the force of the wind seemed as though it would press the breath from his lungs; the hail cut into his face like gunpowder, and his legs sank to the knees in drifted snow. These things did not deter Looey Sing from his purpose, for he began scrambling and fighting his way along towards the near-by woods.

Once he gained their shelter it felt as though he had come out of a world of chaos into one of calm. True, the driving storm found its way there, too, but the wind was tempered, and the hail was filtered by the heavily laden branches. The roar of the wind reached him from high up, but compared with the unprotected stretch of road, it was a haven of silence.

The lack of big drifts made it easier to get along in the woods. Looey Sing picked his course with the certainty born of intimate knowledge through the dark aisles between the trees. Always he was descending, until twenty minutes after he had entered the shelter of the trees he came out at the river's edge.

Even now he did not pause but, turning to the left, began to walk more quickly. His heavy gum shoes gripped the ice without slipping and, close in as he was, the overhanging trees broke the force of the storm.

For another ten minutes he kept along on the ice until he came to a small wood-girdled cove.

Had he been able to see distinctly he would have perceived that the darker patch directly ahead was open water; but its proximity held no terrors for the Celestial.

Too often had his eyes rested on that spot during the day. Swinging along the edge of the little cove the Chinaman came to a pause before a small shed, the door of which took up almost the whole end of the building.

He fumbled in the pocket of his coat for a few minutes, and when his hand emerged it held a long electric flash tube and a key. Taking the tube in his left hand he pressed the switch, revealing a strong hasp on the door, secured by a heavy padlock. Into this he fitted the key.

A moment later the double doors swung open, and before him was a long, heavily-built motorboat.

Its bow was towards him, and between it and the sides of the shed was barely room to walk. It rested on a small framework of wood set on four rimmed, tramway wheels, and these in turn on two rails which passed out under the door, and disappeared in the depths of the black water.

Keeping his light going, Looey Sing made his way along one side of the boat until he reached the stern. In the rear end of the building had been set a tiny winch, the chain of which held boat and wheeled frame in the shed.

The Chinaman crawled in over the stern and, bending, released the iron clasp which held the winch. Almost at once there was the low ramble of the wheels as they moved along the track, the louder rattle of the chain as it unwound from the winch. Each moment the boat gathered speed.

Already the bow was outside, nose pointed towards the water; then the cockpit shot past the door, and the whole affair went rapidly down the incline to the water.

"Jehoshaphat! You are sure some Chink, Looey Sing. I didn't think you'd get here to-night," said the captain, as Looey Sing entered.

A splash in front, an uplifting of the bow, a few icy drops of water in his face, and Looey Sing was afloat with the framework continuing down the submerged track until it should reach the limit of the chain.

Still grasping his light, the Chinaman moved forward to the engine and bent over it. A moment later there was a series of sharp coughs as he swung the fly-wheel. Again he turned it, and the rhythmic hum of the engine followed. Leaping to the tiller, he sat down and bent low.

As the boat gathered speed and sprang onwards through the black stretch of open water, the full force of the wind hit him; the boat struck floe after floe and drove them before her or sheered off quivering; but Looey Sing sat rigid, his eyes peering straight ahead, his whole attitude one of disregard for storm and ice and darkness.

He headed the boat straight down river and, helped by the onrushing tide, he was soon far out in mid-channel. The exhaust of the motor, muffled even on ordinary occasions, was totally lost in the greater roar of the gale. From the shore he was invisible and unheard, though it was unlikely that any other human being was abroad that gale-swept night.

For fully half an hour the motor throbbed unchecked while the boat drove on through the night. He had passed through the Narrows now, and was well down in the wider part of the river.

The red light at Bog Brook had flashed by like a fleeting spark from the devil's engine; the dilapidated old breakwater which lies at the entrance to the Narrows had been invisible, so thick were the snow and sleet.

Still the motionless Celestial bent low, and still his eyes searched the dark stretch of the river ahead. To his left he saw the light of the first lighthouse.

No sooner did he leave it behind than the second on the Canadian side appeared; then suddenly far, far ahead a tiny spark pierced the storm, winked, was gone, only to reappear and disappear again and again.

It was the revolving light on St. Croix Island— the little island where De Monts and Champlain spent the terrible winter of 1604.

Now to his left, with the shore lighthouse behind, a dim black line marked the timbered bank. This, too, was soon lost to view, and there took its place a wider expanse of dark water. He had reached Oak Point, where the narrower part of the river ends, and sweeps abruptly up into the bay of the same name. Then, and only then, did Looey Sing change his course.

Putting the tiller hard over to starboard, he swept on in a great curve around the point, and kept on in his present course until the timber on the shore loomed startlingly close to him; then he set her head straight.

It was quieter in the bay. The storm was now behind him, and in close to the shore the point to his left formed a wind break. The sleet still flung itself at his face, however, and his mittens had been frozen stiff by the flying spray.

For ten minutes he kept on his present course, following the line of the shore until, dead ahead, a single light appeared. It came out of the storm as though careering along on the wings of the wind, but even as the Celestial looked, a darker, bulk appeared beneath it.

Holding the tiller with one hand, Looey Sing bent forward and shut off the engine. The boat, driven onwards by its own impetus, gave more to the tossing waves as its speed lessened; then slower and slower it went until the black bulk ahead grew close, and the nose of the motor-launch gently struck the side of a schooner.

She was anchored in under the lee of the shore, with every sail clewed up and hatches battened down. Certainly she would have created no comment had she been seen, for it was a night to make any ship run for shelter. The only suspicious circumstance was the fact that she should be so far up the river at that time of the year, but that detail had been attended to, if one judged her purpose by her cargo, which was coal, to be discharged at the little town of Red Beach almost across the river on the American side.

Evidently those on the schooner had been on the look-out for the Celestial. Barely had the motor-boat struck the side, when a rope was thrown over, to fall across the gunwales. Looey Sing grasped it, and tied the end to his boat, then, leaping upwards, he caught the side of the schooner, and drew himself over.

Two men were standing on the deck, and without a word they conducted him aft to the small, dingy saloon. A smoky oil lamp lit up the place, and showed them to be white men.

One was tall and gaunt, with smooth-shaven face, and sharp, pointed features—a typical American skipper of the coasting type. The other was short and of a stocky build. What the first lacked in hirsute adornment he made up for.

His face was almost covered by a flaming red beard and moustache, his small eyes peeping forth like those of a weasel. His arms were extraordinarily long, and even under the thick blue serge of his coat showed big and powerful. His legs were short and bowed. Had his beard been black he would have looked not unlike a gorilla.

They both waited until the Celestial had divested himself of his mittens, coat, and cap. While redbeard pushed forward a bottle of whisky and glasses, the taller one spoke.

"Jehoshaphat! Looey Sing, you are sure some Chink! I didn't think you'd get here to-night."

"Me say me come—allee light, me come," answered the Chinaman, pouring out and gulping down about four fingers of the neat spirit.

Then redbeard broke in, and though he addressed his companion as captain, it was evident from his tones that the title was a mere matter of form. Undoubtedly he dominated the other.

"Believe me, captain, we ain't got no time for talk. If Looey Sing wants to get back with his cargo, he will have to hump himself. If this gale gets any worse, he will find himself piled up on the island, and then there will be the devil to pay. I'm gettin' nervous, I am, and the sooner we makes the beach with our legitimate cargo, the better pleased yours truly will be."

"Oh, close your trap before you fall in!" grunted the individual addressed as captain. "The Chink has kept word, and wants a blow before he goes back. If he had been piled up on the shore before he reached here, we might have had a chance to kick."

"Believe me, if he had, yours truly would have been ploughing the drifts on the Canadian side by morning," rumbled the mate.

Looey Sing had sat as impassive as ever all this time, moving only once, and that in order to pour out another drink. Now he looked up?

"You bling them all light?" he asked, looking at the captain.

"Sure as anything you know, Looey," answered the other. "We hit the Bay of Fundy two days ago. Hung about for a bit until nightfall. The motor-launch from St. John turned up sharp on time, and passed over the cargo to us. Gave us a little matter of five hundred tins of opium, too. Then we clamped on all sail, and tried to get up the river before the storm broke, but it caught us from behind this side of Lubec.

"Believe me, all the winds in the Atlantic have sure come to this old river to celebrate Christmas. We were off Red Beach about noon, but beat up and down the river. Signalled we couldn't make the wharf to-night, and would anchor up here. So there you are, Looey, my boy. If you are ready, we will get the cargo out and into your boat."

"I all leady," answered the Celestial. "You bling money?"

"Sure thing," said the captain, "Get the dough out, Reddy," he added, turning to the mate. "Looey wants to see the colour of it before he moves. Thinks we might skin him."

"No, me not tink that," said the Chinaman imperturbably. "Business is business, and Looey Sing allee samee business man."

The mate had opened a big sea-chest while the Celestial had been speaking, and taking out a large canvas bag, tossed it on the table.

"There you are," he rumbled. "Four thousand plunks of the best Canadian greenbacks."

Looey Sing undid the string which held the mouth of the bag together, and took out the contents. They proved be a thick wad of banknotes of all denominations, from five dollars to a hundred dollars. Some were dirty, greasy, and microbe-laden, others new and crisp.

But their condition mattered not to Looey Sing, for the oldest notes received the same caressing attention as his yellow fingers ran through them as did the newer ones. All was grist which came to the Chinaman's mill.

When he had counted them, and verified the amount, he replaced them in the bag, and stuffed it in turn beneath the blue laundryman's jacket which he wore.

"You bling five hundred tins opium?" he said, look up at the Captain.

"Yes. How much do you want for putting that through, you old heathen?"

"Two dollals tin—one tousand dollals."

"Caesar's ghost! Why don't you make it a little more?"

For answer, Looey Sing spread out his hands.

"Two dollals," he said, in a sing-song tone. "No mo', no less. Allee samee last time."

The captain shrugged, knowing the futility of arguing with the Celestial, for Looey Sing's position was unique. He constituted the main link in a long and complicated system of law evasion, and, knowing the full strength of his position, acted accordingly.

The mysterious cargo of which the captain spoke might be passed through many hands until it reached Looey Sing, and after entering American territory, it might pass through many more, but did the Chinaman in the ship's cabin that night refuse to do his part the whole vast system of "underground" commerce would be held up. Consequently, another thousand dollars was counted out to Looey Sing, and these followed the canvas bag beneath his jacket. Then he stood up.

"Now me leady," he said calmly.

"Wait a minute," said the captain, motioning him back to his seat. "We have a special package this time."

He glanced at the mate as he spoke, and that individual departed surily, presumably on some unspoken order.

Looey Sing subsided, and waited.

"It ain't like the others, neither," went on the captain, biting the end off a stogie.

Still the Celestial waited, his face as impassive as ever, though perhaps his eyes had narrowed the barest trifle.

"For Heaven's sake, don't sit there lookin' like a hanged yellow sphinx!" exclaimed the captain, pouring out a drink.

It was very evident that the special package, whatever it might be, was of a different nature from any he had carried before.

"Me wait," was all Looey Sing said.

"I didn't know about it myself," went on the captain hurriedly, "until it was put aboard from the boat which met us in the Bay of Fundy. I refused it at first, for this class of stuff is not to my liking; but Higgins, the mate, persuaded me to take it. The agent for St. John says the New York channels for this class of goods is closed—too risky now—and if we handle the regular cargoes, we must take a certain number of these.

"This one, in particular, is very special stuff, and before I hand it over, let me tell you it's a case clear through to China. It is meant for a mandarin of the Purple Button there, and if any harm comes to it— well"—and the captain sank his voice to a hoarse whisper—"the Brotherhood of the Yellow Beetle will take vengeance; and I guess you know what that means, though I've only got a vague idea myself."

"You talk much, much," said the Celestial, twirling a cigarette in his fingers. "If Blothel-hood Yellow Beetle say clear thlough, you bet Looey Sing obey. What is the package?"

"I guess you had better see it," answered the captain, and at that moment the door opened.

Both he and Looey Sing looked up. At first it seemed as though the bearded mate was the only one to enter, but as he came within the penumbra of the hanging oil lamp, it was seen that he was dragging someone behind him. As he drew close he stood aside, and revealed the slim form of a girl.

Her face was concealed by a heavy veil, and her body was wrapped in a long, capacious coat of squirrel skin; but an intangible something in her pose told of youth, and the tangled masses of fair hair made it seem impossible that aught but beauty could be stamped upon the features beneath the veil.

She was relaxed in attitude, and the support of the mate's arm told the experienced Celestial that she was in a condition of semi-consciousness only, as she had been and would be while in the hands of the underground system. For, be it understood, that a victim in a continual condition of semi-consciousness through drugs is a victim without cognisance of time or place or distance; and with that complicated system this is as it should be.

The mate looked at his chief.

"Did you tell him?"

The captain nodded, and took another drink. "Yes; but, hang it! I don't like it. She's white, and no wife for any purple-buttoned mandarin— whatever in blazes that may be—he's yellow."

"Oh, dry up!" growled the mate disrespectfully. "Do you think the rake off we make out of this is to be picked up every day? Will he take her?"

The captain turned to the Chinaman.

"Will you?" he asked a trifle thickly, for the spirit was beginning to tangle his tongue a trifle. Looey Sing nodded slowly.

"Yes, me take he'. Put he' in the boat."

The mate withdrew with the girl, presumably to do so, and involuntarily the captain heaved a sigh of relief, for he was glad in the first place to get the girl off his hands, and, in the second place, Looey Sing had not, as he expected, asked for extra money for taking her.

The Chinaman rose at that moment, and the captain followed suit. Together they made their way to the deck and across to the side beneath which the motor-boat swung.

The gale had now eased a little, and already patches of star-studded purple were showing overhead as the clouds broke and scudded-along at hurricane speed. The snow and sleet had let up, and the black line of the timbered shore now stood out clear cut and distinct in the frosty night air.

They paused at the side and peered over into the boat below. A solitary figure sat in the stem, though its lines were blurred. They both knew, however, that it was the girl.

Then the trample of feet sounded along the deck, and two sailors appeared, each bearing a small wooden case in their arms. These they lowered into the boat, and returned for more and more, until ten cases in all had been put aboard. It was the opium.

Again the sound of trampling feet came along the deck, this time much louder. A body of men next appeared, marching in single file. They drew up in line before the captain and Looey Sing, and the latter, taking a lantern from the hand of a sailor, walked slowly along the line, inspecting them one by one. There were nineteen in all, and their faces were yellow, their eyes slanted.

They were countrymen of Looey Sing's, bound by the great underground route from England through Canada to the United States— that country which forbids unconditionally the entry of Chinese.

Girl, opium, and Celestials, be it noted, were alike referred to collectively as "cargo," and individually as "packages." Such was another detail of the System. Satisfied with his scrutiny, Looey Sing passed the lantern back with a grunt.

"All light," he said briefly. "Go on!"

The line of men needed no further order. One by one they went over the side and dropped into the boat below. When the last had disappeared, Looey Sing went back to the cabin and donned his fur coat and cap; then, stuffing his hands into his mittens, he passed out and over the side.

A moment later, the rhythmic hum of the motor came upwards, the boat swung and headed for the point. Ten minutes later it had gone, not even the muffled sound of the exhaust reaching the schooner. When it had quite disappeared, the captain and mate returned to the saloon, and began an attack on the whisky-bottle.

They had done a pretty stroke of business—in fact, it was only one of many strokes which they had done. Five hundred tins of opium and nineteen Chinamen had gone through, not to speak of the slim girl, who had completed that stage of her long journey through to China, there to become the wife of a yellow mandarin whom she had never seen.

Yes, all things considered, the captain, the mate, and the crew of the schooner looked forward to a happy Christmas Day on the morrow.

All during that cold, spray-flying trip Looey Sing's "cargo" sat hunched up in the bow and amidships, shivering and silent. As for the fur-clad girl who sat beside him in the stern, she gave not the slightest sign that she was aware of her change of quarters. Only a low, muffled moan issued at intervals from behind the thick veil. Undoubtedly, though in a semi-comatose condition, some subconscious feeling was causing her to suffer.

Looey Sing himself neither spoke nor shifted his position, except to move the tiller as occasion demanded it. What might be behind those inscrutable eyes no man might tell. Not even his own countrymen had the temerity to address him. To them he was for the time being as a sovereign lord, holding their destinies in his wrinkled yellow hands.

Back along the course he had come went the Celestial. A jutting point on the American side of the river shut off the view of the revolving light on the island, now far behind. One lighthouse had been passed, and soon the steady flame of the other was dead ahead.

As the boat swept onwards, nosing the still outrushing tide, the old breakwater which before had been invisible, came into view.

It, on the one side, and the lighthouse on the other, sped past; then they struck the Narrows where still burned the red light of Bog Brook. A few moments only, and they were in the wide river, again heading for the wooded cove where stood the boat-shed.

On reaching the entrance, Looey Sing cut off the motor and let the boat drive in under its own impetus, until it gently nosed the slip, quivered slightly, and lay quiet, rising and falling gently on the little waves of its own making. A low, guttural command sent the nineteen Celestials over the bow, and another order set them at work pulling on the rope.

While they held the boat steady, Looey Sing picked up the girl as though she were a child, and carrying her along to the bow, passed her over. Leaping over himself, he entered the shed and began winding up the winch. Slowly the wheeled frame came out of the depths, until its grooved cross-pieces received the keel of the boat; then frame and boat together began to move upwards along the tracks.

Five minutes, and they were back in their original place in the shed, the doors had been closed and locked, and Looey Sing stood on the slip outside surveying his "cargo." A moment only, and he signed for the girl to be passed to him.

With her in his arms, he uttered a low grunt, and struck off along the ice edging the river's bank. He turned in at the point where he had before left the woods, and without pausing, walked swiftly along, leaving the others to scramble along after as best they could.

Before breaking from the cover of the woods into the open, he stopped and surveyed the snow-clad stretch between him and the shack. Not a sound of man or beast broke the silence of the cold, frosty night; but just as he was beginning to move forward again, a silvery note floated faintly to their ears from far up the river. It was the church bells in the town above, ringing out the summons to the

Christmas Eve service.

Not until the last chime had died away did Looey Sing advance, and if the bells of the strange gods had struck any deep chord in his nature, he gave no sign.

The rear room of the shack was exactly as he had left it. The coals in the stove now burned red, and the Celestials crowded about it, glad of the welcome heat.

Poor wretches! What hardships and suffering they truly pass through in order to reach the forbidden land where every day will be a golden day—so they think—and in a short time they will be able to return to the land of their sacred ancestors with wealth and position, there to live the lazy days of the lotus eater.

Looey Sing gave them little time to thaw their stiff joints in the rear room. Placing the girl in a chair, he moved over to a corner and rolled away a barrel of flour which stood on end. A small trap-door was disclosed, and this he lifted up. Then he signed to the Celestials, who descended one by one. Looey Sing himself followed.

The cellar beneath proved to be a bare, stonewalled room formed by the foundations of the building. In the centre stood a small stove, and along the sides were ranged several rude benches. It was windowless, and how it received ventilation was a mystery.

Looey Sing pointed to a heap of wood and coal on the floor beside the stove, and then to the benches.

"Remain here until I come, unworthy pigs!" he said gutturally, in Chinese. "There is wood and coal for warmth. There are benches for rest. I will bring food when I come. And, by all your unworthy ancestors, let me hear no sound!"

With that he ascended the stairs again and closed the trapdoor, rolling the barrel of flour back into place. This done, he approached the girl, and drew her chair nearer the fire. Swiftly he moved to the cupboard in the wall and hung up his coat and cap.

After, he drew out several dishes and jars, and set to work to prepare food and drink for the girl. When he had finished, he went over to her and lifted the veil she wore until her features were visible.

The fair promise of her hair was not belied. Her features, were small and perfect, and though she was white as death, cold pallor lent to rather than detracted from the appealing sweetness of the face. Her eyes were closed, but one could imagine them deep blue wells containing all the promise and softness of the morning sky.

Looey Sing wasted no time in surveying her features. He had work to do, and it must be done. It was no easy matter feeding her, but after some time he accomplished it. Then he lifted her up and laid her on a couch, drawing a heavy rug over her.

With a last look around, he closed the door of the store, and departed for the outer shop. There he spread out several rugs on the rude counter, and soon dead silence reigned over the apparently deserted shack of Looey Sing, laundryman and general storekeeper.

● ●　　●　　●

Twenty-four hours later, when all the Christian world was celebrating the festivities of the Great Day, a long "double-runner" sled drew up in front of Looey Sing's.

Barely had it come to a stop when the door opened, a dark figure shot out and into the dark shelter of its covered top. Another and another followed, until nineteen in all had gone. Then came a twentieth, bearing a burden wrapped in fur.

The burden was placed in the sled, the figure which had borne it spoke a few words to the driver, and the four powerful horses which drew the sled started off on their roundabout journey by lonely country roads to the next stopping-place, which this time would be on the American side.

The door of Looey Sing's shop slammed behind him, and he returned to the rear room, there to sit hunched over the fire, smoking his eternal yellow cigarettes, gazing into the red coals—seeing what pictures, thinking what thoughts, Heaven only knows.

END OF PROLOGUE.

THE STORY.

Looey Sing found it a hard task feeding the subconscious girl, but at last he accomplished it. (*Page 6.*)

THE usually austere appearance of Sexton Blake's consulting-room at Baker Street presented a distinctly gala appearance. The desk, the chairs, the table, and even the floor were littered with a varied array of books, leather articles, silver and gold cigarette and cigar-cases (some studded with glittering diamonds or sapphires), and all the thousand and one things which go to make up the Christmas tribute to that difficult individual—a bachelor.

It was Christmas Eve, and the presents had been arriving by post and messengers all day.

Tinker sat half buried under an avalanche in one corner, endeavouring to fit a heavily-studded collar on the disdainful Pedro, who eyed the blaze of the distant fire with a longing eye. Blake himself was seated at his desk, gazing about him with an air of helpless bewilderment.

Each year the same thing happened, and each year he became lost in his own rooms, futilely hoping that something would turn up to prevent the same thing the following year—a something which as yet seemed to successfully evade the harassed bachelor.

Mrs. Bardell boldly declared what he needed was a wife—a nice, homely body who would keep him in order, and with her sewing— But she never got farther than that. Blake always waved her away.

Though only four o'clock in the afternoon, it was already dark and cold outside. A few wet flakes of snow were trying to make a show in the midst of a drizzling rain. Served by the acoustic properties of the street, the constant bleat of motor-horns, and the heavy ramble of 'buses came to them through the fast-closed windows.

Wet or no wet, it was Christmas Eve in London, and Londoners must be served.

Certainly the cosy, though littered, consulting-room was a pleasant retreat on such a day.

Blake had been sunk in reverie, his eyes gazing unseeingly into the mounting flames of the fire. He was roused by Tinker giving up his attempts on the unreciprocative Pedro's neck, and as the lad rolled the dog over and over in a rough-and-tumble, Blake turned back to his desk with the faintest of sighs.

What had caused the touch of sadness in his thoughts it is hard to say. Perhaps he was thinking of the misery which must exist even at such a time when goodwill reigns supreme; perhaps he was thinking of the past, and of some happy moment now gone for ever; perhaps he was thinking that, with all his work and all his interests, even with Tinker and Pedro he was just a trifle lonely.

Whatever it was, he cast it from his mind, and an introspective smile crossed his face as he picked up the pile of cards which lay on the desk before him.

They were cards of good wishes and seasonable greetings from every part of the globe, and had Blake cared to speak, he could have told you that almost all of them had their inception in some past deed which he had performed for the sender.

What a volume of memoirs they would have made!

There were cards from Japan, China, and the mountain-girded Tibet; cards from Honolulu, Fiji, and Easter Island; cards from Australia, New Zealand, and one even from an expedition in the Antarctic; cards from South Africa, Mombassa, Khartoum, and Timbuctu; from South America, Mexico, and the West Indies; cards from the United States, Canada, and Labrador; an avalanche from the British Isles, and a towering pile from every country in Europe, most of which bore a coronet.

What stirring moments they recalled; what deep currents of plot and intrigue and crime; what potential forces brought clashing together in terrific collision and mortal combat; what depths of smiles and tears—of joy and of sorrow!

Tinker, having finished his impromptu struggle with Pedro, in which the bloodhound got the worst of it, for the simple reason that he was too lazy to struggle, looked up from where he sat on the prostrate animal.

"I say, guv'nor!" he said, "this is a bit of all right, isn't it? No case for two days, and it looks as though we would eat the old gobbler in peace to-morrow."

"I hope so," smiled Blake absently. "A little spell of idleness at this time of the year will do us both good. By the way, if you will go to your room and look on the table, you will find a trifling remembrance which I got for you."

Tinker grinned with a strange shyness.

"If you will make the same journey to your room, you will find something on the table, too," he said, as he rose.

Blake smiled and stood up.

"All right, my lad, we will both go and see what inspiration we received."

They departed, each his different way—Tinker along the corridor to his room, which was next to the laboratory, and Blake through the dressing-room, which led off from the consulting-room. Less than a minute later they both returned. Blake's smile had widened, and Tinker was in convulsions.

In their hands each held a large Morocco leather case containing a silver-mounted Colt's automatic revolver of exactly the same calibre.

"Well, if this isn't about the limit," stuttered Tinker, when he succeeded in getting his breath. "I got one for you and you got one for me. I gave you one because I heard you say the trigger of your old one was wearing a bit."

"And I yours, my lad, because you lost your own the last time we were in South America, and I knew you hated that old six-shooter you carry. Never mind, as it happened, we both got what we needed and would put off buying through hating to break in a new gun."

Simultaneously they both took the revolvers from the cases, and worked the ejectors with experienced fingers. While they were so engaged, a knock came at the door, and Mrs. Bardell entered to announce a visitor. Blake frowned impatiently, and was on the point of telling her he could see no one, when the caller himself appeared in the door. The frown left Blake's face instantly, as he recognised who it was, and Tinker grinned in welcome.

"Well, well, Mr. Kennedy come in," said Blake cordially, as he advanced and held out his hand. "It is a surprise to see you in London at this time of the year."

The man addressed as Kennedy strode into the room, and shook hands first with Blake and then with Tinker. He was a man of medium size, a trifle stocky in build. His chin was cleanshaven, and a close-cropped sandy moustache hid his mouth. His nose was big and straight, his eyes keen and humorous. A pleasing personality altogether, and the last man one would pick as the most brilliant private detective in the United States.

"You can just bet I wouldn't be here if it wasn't necessary," he laughed, taking the seat Blake indicated. "Great Scott! You are upset here. All this array would make a tempting haul, Mr. Blake."

Blake opened a box of cigars and passed it over. "To tell you the truth, I don't know what to do with the stuff," he said. "I am seriously thinking of starting an anti-Christmas present league, with myself as president."

"Yes," put in Tinker, "and he's the worst of the lot himself. We have despatched enough merchandise from here this week to stock a good sized general store."

After a few more light remarks, in which the joke of the revolvers was explained to the appreciative American, Blake glanced at his visitor quizzically.

"Did you come to get any information?" he asked.

"Well, not exactly that," answered Kennedy. "To tell you the truth, I came for a bit more. I want your co-operation in a case on which I am working. I have been digging into a certain matter for well over six months now, and honestly, I am up against a brick wall as solid as the Gizeh pyramid."

Blake knit his brows.

"Six months," he said reminiscently. "I don't seem to recall any big crime which took place in New York six months ago."

"And you wouldn't, for the simple reason that everything has been kept mum," answered Kennedy. "It isn't a crime, strictly speaking. It is a colossal fraud, and I have been retained by the Secret Service Department to ferret out matters. I have come over here, because I feel that the affair has its inception on this side. The finished perfection of its operation proves that."

"I am afraid I don't understand."

"You will in a few minutes, if you say you will join me."

"As a matter of fact, I had intended taking nothing on until the New Year. My own affairs have been sadly neglected of late, and coming on the end of the year, I should like to get everything fixed up. However, if it is a matter of exceptional interest professionally, I don't mind considering it."

"I guess you will find it interesting enough from a professional point of view," remarked Kennedy. "At any rate, I will run my chances and tell you the details. I will give them to you exactly as they were handed to me; then, if you are interested, I will give you an outline of everything I have done during the past six months."

Blake nodded.

"Very well," he said quietly. "I can at least promise you my closest attention."

Tinker drew closer in order to hear, and after deliberately knocking the ash from his cigar, Kennedy began:

"I was in Washington," he said, "just a little over six months ago, when I received a wire from the head of the Secret Service Department in New York to come on at once in order to take up a special case. I turned over the work I was on to an assistant, and caught the train that same night. I reached New York at ten o'clock, and at ten-fifteen was closeted with the chief.

"You will recall that just over a year ago, there was a big shake up in the Customs and Immigration services at New York and Boston, and as a result, the inspection became of a much more rigorous nature than it had been previously. Though the reason was not made public, the shake up occurred owing to the fact that large numbers of Chinese were slipping into the country by way of those two ports.

"Of course, we know a good few get in over the Mexican and Western Canadian borders, but only bribery could get them in through ports like New York and Boston. After six months it was found that, regardless of the care taken at those two ports, the Chinese colony in each was increasing.

"A thorough investigation proved conclusively that they were not getting in by either of them. The question was how was it being worked? That was when they sent for me. Now, Mr. Blake, if you are interested in the subject, I will tell you what I have done."

"By all means proceed," said Blake. "I am always interested in matters Celestial."

"Well, as soon as I was in possession of all the facts the chief could give me, I went along to my hotel and got out a map. I guess I studied that in detail until daybreak, trying to put my finger on the weak spot. I couldn't seem to locate it, however, and the next day decided to try a bit of quiet detective work.

"I got myself appointed as Special Immigration Officer with unfettered authority and a roving commission.

"The first place I made for was New Orleans. I put in a fortnight there; then I moved on to Mobile. In that way I worked up along the coast, putting in a week or a fortnight at each port, as the case seemed to warrant. I hit on a few curious things, but had worked clear up to

New York without hitting a single thing that said 'Chink.'

"I put in a solid month in New York, and from there went to Boston. Nothing doing. On to Portland, Bangor and Machias—still nothing doing. From Machias I moved on to Eastport, and from there up the St. Croix River to Calais. And though I know, as sure as I am sitting here, that the game is being worked through some point at which I touched, I struck not the faintest sign of what I was after. I was in a quandary for fair.

"That was a month ago, and I then decided to try Canada. I got back into civilian clothes and crossed the border. I mixed with all classes, and must say the officials on that side gave me all the aid in their power. Finally, I decided that whether the Chinese were coming direct from the sea through one of our ports, or whether they were getting in via Canada, the starting point of the system was on this side. I wired the chief I was coming over, and here I am."

"How about the six months during which you have been working on the matter?" asked Blake. "Has the influx stopped at all?"

"Not on your life. Why hang it, it has increased if anything."

"H'm! They seem to have hit on a pretty clever system in order to defy the law, under your very nose."

"That is exactly what has put me on my mettle. I have shelved everything else, and I vow I will not touch another case until I unravel this riddle. At the same time, I want your help if you will give it to me."

"I must confess the affair interests me keenly," rejoined Blake slowly. "It just happens, that for some time past I have been up against a Chinese organisation myself, and although I had an intimate knowledge of that subtle race before, I have certainly learned a good many new facts concerning them. If you think my assistance will be of value to you—why I don't mind joining you."

"Put it there," cried the American, thrusting out his hand. "You have sure taken a big weight off my mind. You know all the wrinkles on this side of the pond, and if that yellow riddle has its inception here, between us we ought to hit it."

Blake smiled as he shook hands; then he grew grave again. "Have you no clue of any description?"

"Absolutely none. I tell you, Mr. Blake, it is as though they dropped from the sky. In fact, I even went so deep into the matter as to seriously consider the theory that they might be coming over by aeroplane, but a thorough investigation made that end in smoke. They are getting in regularly, and once they reach the security of the big Chinese colony in any of the large cities, it is hopeless to dislodge them. That is all I know."

"It is certainly a matter which will require a good deal of thought before we make a move over here," remarked Blake. "I think, however, if there is anything like that having its genesis here, we will eventually discover it. I have a most intimate acquaintance with the haunts and habits of the Chinese in this metropolis. For my part, I hardly think we shall find what we seek in London, however.

"For one reason, my own investigations have taken me through Limehouse a good deal lately, and I must surely have discovered some trace of what you mention, had it existed. The biggest proof of such a thing is the crowd which patronises the different opium and gambling dens. If these crowds keep changing all the time, it is safe to assume that something is going on; but if one sees the same faces week after week, it is a safe bet that their operations are being carried on locally. And for some time past the latter has been the case here.

"No, Mr. Kennedy, in my opinion, if the beginning of the system is in England, we stand much more chance of striking something suspicious in places such as Cardiff or Liverpool than in London. Please understand that is purely a tentative theory, and is subject to correction."

The American had followed Blake's every word with the closest attention. When the latter had finished Kennedy spoke quickly.

"By ginger! Your argument is sound, Mr. Blake. Now I had the idea that the game started here in London, but the more I think of it the more I am inclined to agree with you. Cardiff and Liverpool both have big Chinese districts, I know, and from what I have heard, they are pretty tough, too."

"They are not as bad as the river front of Canton or the water stretches of Shanghai," answered Blake; "but I assure you they are quite odious enough for this country. I am sorry I cannot go into the matter further with you to-day, Mr. Kennedy, but I have an appointment for dinner this evening. However, I should be very glad to see you to-morrow morning, and then we can discuss things as well as arrange a plan of campaign. Besides, I should like to turn the matter over in my mind to-night. Something might occur to me."

"By all means do so, Mr. Blake," replied the other rising. "I myself am due to dine out tonight. How will ten o'clock in the morning suit you? I feel guilty, I assure you, breaking up your Christmas in this manner."

"Oh, that is all right!" smiled Blake, getting to his feet. "Ten o'clock in the morning will suit me excellently. Tinker, just jot that appointment down."

When Kennedy had departed, Blake returned to the desk, and was just about to sit down, when Mrs. Bardell again entered, and informed him that a lady wished to see him. The frown of irritation again furrowed Blake's brow, but he curtly bade the housekeeper to show her in.

He sat impatiently tapping the desk with the end of a pencil, and so silently did the visitor enter, that not until Tinker coughed, did Blake become aware that she was in the room.

As his eyes rested on her face, he rose at once, and bowed.

"Won't you sit down?" he said quietly.

As the woman inclined her head, and walked across the room, it was easy to see what had inspired the gentle quietude of Blake's tone. She was a tall, well proportioned woman, of middle age, or more. Her simple, though rich, costume of black, topped by a small delicately-turned hat, spoke of taste, and the means to gratify it.

Her carriage was perfect, and her clear-cut features were those of a woman who must have ranked as a noted beauty in her younger days. Her head was poised on her shoulders with a dignity almost akin to haughtiness; her whole bearing was proud and reserved.

In her eyes, however, Blake's keen gaze had read deep tragedy, and from his knowledge of human nature he knew only too well how serious it must be to make a woman of her stamp confide in an outsider, even though that outsider were Blake.

A glance sent Tinker out of the room, and when the door had closed softly behind him, Blake turned to his visitor.

"You wished to see me upon some matter?" he asked gravely.

His visitor bowed her head.

"You are Mr. Blake?"

"Yes."

"I will first tell you who I am," she went on.

As she spoke, she passed over a card to Blake, and his eyes widened the barest trifle as he read the name engraved upon it. It was: "The Duchess of Carrisbrooke."

It must indeed be a matter of urgency to send her Grace to see him on Christmas Eve of all times.

Blake laid the card on his desk, and glanced up. "I judge that you are in a difficulty of some description," he said quietly. "If it is my advice you have come to seek, I am at your service."

The woman studied him for a few minutes in silence; then she leaned forward.

"Mr. Blake, I do not know you, but I come to you at the instigation of my husband. He has told me that not only are you an investigator of crimes and mysteries, but that you are a chivalrous gentleman as well."

Blake bowed, but made no reply.

"For that reason," continued the duchess, "I have come to confide in you, and tell you what has caused both the duke and myself the greatest anxiety during the past fortnight."

Blake held up his hand.

"Pardon me, your Grace. Before you confide in me, I should like to say something."

"By all means do so."

"It is this. What your trouble is I have not the faintest idea, but if I am to listen to you, and give you the benefit of any experience I may have, I must insist upon absolute frankness on your part. Only by receiving your full confidence, can I be of use to you."

"It is hard to tell you everything, Mr. Blake, but I promise you I shall reserve nothing."

"Then I am quite ready," responded Blake.

"To begin with, Mr. Blake," said the duchess, "You may know of the famous Carrisbrooke pride, and how it causes any member of the family to flinch from publicity. Two weeks ago something occurred which upset us dreadfully, but for a solid fortnight we have carried on the investigation ourselves, owing to our desire to keep it from the public. That occurrence happened while we were in Cardiff.

"At that time, my husband, my daughter, and myself went to Cardiff, where my husband was to attend a directors' meeting of which he was chairman. We stayed at the Hotel North, where we always put up when there. On our very first evening there, I had a frightful headache, and retired to my room about seven in the evening. My husband and daughter went down to dinner alone.

"After dinner, my daughter ran up and kissed me good-bye,

saying she was going to walk along with her father to the offices where he was to attend a meeting that evening. As it was less than three blocks from the hotel, I did not feel nervous about her returning alone, for she had done the same thing scores of times.

"As the evening passed on, and she did not return, I began to feel a trifle worried, but felt satisfied she had remained there, intending not to return until her father did.

"About half past nine I dozed off, and did not waken until I heard my husband in his room, which adjoined mine. I called to him, and he came in at once. I asked him why Sybil had not come in to see me before going to her room. He looked at me in surprise, and said he had no idea, that he hadn't seen her since she left him at the offices about a quarter past eight.

"It took us about ten minutes to discover the drift of each others remarks, but when we did, it began to dawn upon us that I had seen nothing of her since just before dinner, and that he had not since a little after eight. At my request, he rang for my daughter's maid. When she appeared, I questioned her, but she said positively she had not seen her mistress since she had dressed for dinner. She thought, as I did, that she was with her father.

"By then we were terribly anxious, but it seemed that she must be about the hotel. I sent the maid down to the office to search the lounge and writing-room, but there were no traces of her. I myself went to her room, but met with the same result there. My husband had also gone to the office, and as discreetly as possible was prosecuting further inquiries there. The commissionaire at the door stated positively that he remembered her going out with the duke, but that she had not come in since. He was on duty all the evening, and must have seen her had she done so. I was nearly frantic.

"My husband got on the 'phone, and called up his fellow directors. They came round at once, and after binding them to secrecy, he told them what had occurred. A search party was organised at once. All night until daybreak they scoured the city, but without result. It was only too evident now that something of a serious nature had happened.

"It was when they were returning at dawn that the first and only clue was found. It was between the offices and the hotel, that one of the search party found a soiled white, evening glove in the gutter. I recognised it instantly as one my daughter had worn. This proved she had come back that way after leaving her father, but she had never reached the hotel.

"Since then, we have been working day and night. Our most trusted friends have assisted us, and the search has been carried on, not only in Cardiff, but in Liverpool, London, and half-a-dozen other places. The police have been searching also with a full description of her, but they have discovered nothing. In addition we have advertised in every English and Continental paper offering a reward of fifty thousand pounds for her safe return. But each channel has led to a blank wall.

"From that day to this, we have seen nothing of her, and heard nothing of her, with the exception of the finding of her glove. My husband would have come, but he has broken down, and was compelled to take to his bed.

"That, Mr. Blake, is the story, without any reservations of any description whatever. It is needless for me to say if you can be of any assistance to me, you will find my gratitude of a deep nature."

Blake had listened to her story with the closest attention. It had been easy enough to see that each word was a stab of agony to the proud woman, but her mother-love had overcome her dread of the conventions, and now, even if publicity were demanded in order to get back her daughter, she would face it with a brave face, though her heart might crumple up from the arrows of a harsh world, which is prone to revel in the troubles of their fellows.

For a matter of two minutes, Blake sat turning over in his mind the story she had told him; then he leaned back.

"I remember reading the advertisements which you placed in the papers," he said quietly. "Pardon me, but I suppose your daughter was in love with no one of whom you and your husband did not approve?"

"No—decidedly not. She had never been troubled by her affections. If she had, I must have known, for she was perfectly frank with me in every way."

"Of course," went on Blake, determined to probe each point to the bottom, "in a case of this kind, your Grace, we must not look for a clue only in the present, but examine past events as well. Therein we may discover some apparently trivial thing, which, on analysis, will prove to be the keynote of the mystery. I do not say this is invariably the case, but it is more often so than not. For that reason, I am going to ask you to give me in a very few words a resume of your daughter's life during, say, the past four years. By the way, how old is she?"

"She is just twenty. Four years ago when she was sixteen, she went to Paris, to the same school which I attended when a girl. Then she returned to London, and made her debut, being presented at Court that year. That season we spent in town. From there we went to Cowes, and from Cowes to our Scottish estates for the shooting. The winter we spent at Nice, and in the spring spent a month in Paris before returning to London.

"On our return, my husband was given a diplomatic mission to China, and it was decided that my daughter and myself should go with him. That was a year ago. We went through to Hong Kong, and from there to Pekin. For three months we stayed in Pekin, and only reached England in July, as we had loitered in Ceylon on the way back. Then we went to Scotland, and from there to Cardiff, where she disappeared."

"And in all that period of time—think very carefully, please—there was nothing of any description whatever which brought your daughter before your immediate horizon more than usual?"

The duchess, knit her brows, and studied the carpet.

"I shall endeavour to think if there was," she said.

Blake did not hurry her, and not for several minutes did she look up.

"I have gone over the whole four years, Mr. Blake, and beyond one little thing which occurred, I can think of nothing. Moreover, this occurrence, in a way, had nothing to do with my daughter—that is to say, it was not of her making."

"Ah! I should be glad to hear what it was if you don't mind," said Blake imperturbably.

"It was while we were in Pekin. There, owing to the diplomatic nature of my husband's business, we had to entertain and be entertained by a good many of the native Chinese government officials.

"When we had been in Pekin about a month, my daughter complained that one of them—a Dr. Li-Fuang—had made himself obnoxious to her by attempting to pay her some attention. Not caring to have any unpleasantness, we simply arranged that she should attend no more dinners or entertainments. She spoke once afterwards of having met him in the gardens, and though he had been the model of

31

politeness, she said she was frightened of him. After that, she did not mention the matter again for the reason, I imagine, that she did not meet him.

"That is the only occurrence during the past four years which could be classed as abnormal, and even that is a mere trifle. If you had not seemed to attach such importance to even a trivial matter, I do not know that I ever should have recalled it again."

Blake drew a pad of paper towards him without replying. Picking up a pencil, he jotted down a few notes over which he pondered for some time, while his visitor watched him anxiously.

Finally, he looked up.

"I must confess there seems little during the past four years upon which to build," he said briefly. "At the same time, every item is of value, and if that is all we can only govern ourselves accordingly. I don't mind saying, your Grace, that from a professional point of view, the case presents many difficulties, caused chiefly, by your delay in coming to me. You can rest assured that if your daughter was kidnapped by force, there is a daring brain behind it all, for the average man would think twice before striking so high.

"Of course, it may be that her kidnappers had no idea of her identity, but I do not think that is the case. Were it so, it would mean only another case of a young girl disappearing into the maw of those creatures who prey upon society, and not one of them exists, but would jump at the chances to return her for the enormous reward offered, particularly since you specified that no questions would be asked. No, it seems to point to a certain knowledge on the part of the abductors. At first, I was inclined to think the contrary, but we have had visible proof that even fifty thousand would not tempt them.

"That means it is your daughter whom they want—not money. That being so, there must be a powerful motive behind it all. Once we get our fingers on that it will not be hard to trace the perpetrators, for the motive of any given deed, if strong enough, inevitably points to the perpetrators of the deed, no matter how skilful they may be in covering their tracks.

"In a matter of this description the police are useless during the earlier stages of the investigation. Owing to the great lapse of time which has taken place between her disappearance and your coming to me many of the clues which then existed are certain to be obliterated by now. However, so strong is the evidence of great motive that something may still remain from which a start may be made.

"It just happens that I am entering upon a case which in a remote way runs parallel to this affair, for the points of investigation begin at the same places where your case must be taken up. Owing to that fact, I am prepared to accept your commission, and do what I can towards recovering your daughter, though, mind you, I do not want you to build too much on my ability to do so.

"That is all I can say at present, your Grace. Needless to say, you have my profound sympathy in your trouble, and I can promise you no pains shall be spared to return her to you safe and sound."

The duchess breathed deeply and held out her hand. The cold repression of the face had gone down before the swelling sorrow of the mother, and the fine eyes were drenched with unshed tears.

"How can I thank you, Mr. Blake?" she said chokingly. "She— Sybil—is every thing in the world to her father and me. Her strange disappearance has driven me nearly frantic, and my husband, though he tries to keep up before me, is slowly breaking under the suspense and anxiety."

Blake pressed her hand sympathetically. He made no reply, knowing silence under the circumstances was best.

As the duchess rose to depart she again held out her hand.

Facing as she was, her eyes rested on the desk, from which Blake had also risen. Grasping her fingers, he was about to make some sympathetic remark, when a wide look of utter incredulity in her eyes caused him to turn and follow her gaze to where it rested on the desk. Unconsciously, he was still holding her hand.

As for the duchess, she seemed utterly oblivious of the present, and in this fashion they both looked at the same object.

In itself the thing at which they gazed was not out of the ordinary. It was a small framed sketch of a head done in bold, heavy lines. As a work of art, it had perhaps no particular merit; but as a study in the utter impassivity of which the human mask is capable it was a masterpiece. Barely a dozen lines were there in all, but the bold, heavy sweep of the few which existed portrayed the full face of a Celestial.

His forehead was high and noble; the eyes, slant-set wells of inscrutable wisdom; the nose almost European in the thin, aristocratic turn of the nostrils; the mouth a paradoxical mixture of kindliness and cruelty, of decision and indulgence, the chin bold and obstinate; the head a masterpiece from a master mould.

It was the head of the thinker, the student, the leader, the unyielding dictator, and yet the head of the noble, the aristocrat, and the kindly homemaker.

To Blake it was the head of one of the strongest men against whom he had ever been pitted, the head of a fanatic to whom life was of no real value, and yet the head of a man honest in his purpose; the head of Wu Ling, Prince of the Royal blood of China, descendant of the ancient and noble Ming Dynasty, one time claimant to the Chinese throne, privileged wearer of the Royal saffron, and present head of that colossal organisation which was the greatest menace the white races had ever known—the Brotherhood of the Yellow Beetle.

Somewhat surprised at the interest of the duchess in the picture, he turned and faced her, only to find her eyes meeting his.

"Where—where did you get that picture, Mr. Blake?" she asked hesitatingly.

"That?" he returned lightly. "I sketched that myself from memory, your Grace. It is the face of a man against whom I have been pitted on several occasions, and, I might add, the face of one of the ablest men living to-day."

She nodded slowly.

"I—I know him, Mr. Blake."

"You know him?" he echoed, in surprise.

"Yes. It is Dr. Li-Fuang, whom we met in Pekin."

"Impossible!" exclaimed Blake, knitting his brows. "His name is Wu Ling—Prince Wu Ling. He is one of the few privileged wearers of the yellow."

"Then I am doubly sure, Mr. Blake, for once— only once— when my husband and I entertained a small party of Chinese of high rank, Dr. Li-Fuang wore a yellow tunic."

Blake bent forward suddenly.

"Tell me, your grace, did you notice his hands?"

"Yes."

"And on them did you see a large yellow topaz of a particularly deep colour?"

"I did, for the simple reason that it is so noticeable."

"Then it is, indeed, Wu Ling," muttered Blake, dropping her hand, and beginning to pace up and down the room. "This coincidence is more than important, your Grace. It has caused a seemingly trivial occurrence which happened to your daughter in Pekin to assume proportions of the greatest magnitude in reference to her disappearance. Is it possible—is it possible that he is the man? No—no, I can't believe it, and yet—"

Still muttering to himself, he swung sharply round, and came to a stop before her.

"This discovery, your Grace, has started an entirely fresh trend of thought in my mind. If, on consideration, it proves to be of the nature I think, then, indeed, is the case a difficult one. If Wu Ling and Dr. Li-Fuang are one and the same, and I must confess it seems so—then I shall need all my resources, physical and mental, to ferret out the truth of the problem. If he is, then the abduction of your daughter has some deeper purpose than mere possession. It would mean that she was intended as a hostage, or there—"

Blake paused, for he did not care to voice the thought which came to him—namely, that she might well be intended as the wife of one of Wu Ling's numerous lieutenants, who had seen her and admired her, and for whom Wu Ling had pulled one of the numerous strings he possessed in order to secure her.

His own obnoxious attentions to her in Pekin might have been only an attempt to worm himself into her confidence in order to pump her regarding the true nature of the duke's diplomatic mission, for Wu Ling was a man who believed in knowing the other man's hand before he laid any of his own cards on the table.

Of one thing Blake was certain. He knew Wu Ling, did not wish her for himself. The prince's nature was too cold and austere for that.

So exercised was Blake over the discovery, and so anxious was he to devote his mind to the contemplation and analysis of the different points presented, that he made his adieux to the duchess as brief as possible, promising her that he would communicate with her on the morrow.

When she was gone he called Tinker, and ordered the lad to get down the Index. That done, he sat down and rapped out:

"Get me also my tabular analysis of the 'Mysterious Disappearances of Young Girls' during the past twelve months. Turn up the section dealing with Continental and eastern traffic."

Tinker obeyed at once, and for a solid hour Blake pored over a mass of facts and figures which he had compiled from cases of his own, as well as from information furnished him by his friend

Inspector Thomas, of Scotland Yard.

At the end of that time he pushed the book from him and rose.

"Seven o'clock, my lad. Just time to dress if we are to keep our appointment to dine with Mademoiselle Yvonne at eight."

"I am sorry, mademoiselle, but I cannot permit it. You might fall into their clutches yourself, and—well, I——, I——" For once in his life, Blake was at a loss for words.

THE SECOND CHAPTER   THE DINNER AT YVONNE'S—BILLIARDS— BLAKE TELLS YVONNE ABOUT THE TWO CASES—YVONNE DECIDES TO HELP—IN CARDIFF

BLAKE and Tinker, with Pedro at their heels, left the Baker Street apartments at ten minutes to eight sharp.

The chauffeur, who was rarely used by either of them, was at the kerb in the big grey car, and, in view of the rain and snow which still fell, the top had been drawn over and the side curtains lowered.

Blake ordered the man to drive to an address at Queen Anne's Gate, and sank back in silence, still pondering on the remarkable facts which had come to his notice that day.

Mademoiselle Yvonne had been living at Queen Anne's Gate ever since the memorable affair of "The Mystery of Walla-Walla."

How she met and yielded to Blake's conditions at that time will be recalled by those who followed the case. Since then she and her uncle (Graves) had been living quietly, and a pleasant intimacy had grown up between them and Baker Street.

True, she had more than once been on the wrong side of the strict demands of the law, and more than once Blake had been forced to stretch out a stern hand in order to curb her intentions.

From time to time he had attempted to impress ideas of conformity with the law upon the quixotic girl; but her laughing eyes had only met his with a provoking inattention which had routed all his well-marshalled arguments.

For the time being he rested content in the strangely happy moments he passed there, and, though he did not attempt to analyse the reason, he knew in his heart that did his visits stop for any reason it would mean something big going out of his life.

Tinker had become almost as frequent a visitor as Blake, and as for Pedro—well, the heavily-studded collar, which in the afternoon he had pretended to hold in contempt, and which now he wore with every evidence of pride, had been Yvonne's Christmas gift to the big fellow.

Even in the early days of her remarkable career, when the world, not knowing of the deep motive which had inspired her outrages on society, called her an adventuress, Pedro and she had always been warm friends.

If she still entertained the same deep love for Blake she managed to conceal it from him; but at night, in the privacy of her own room, where the mask of convention was dropped, the sketch of the detective, which hung on the wall, looked down on many hours of suffering as she lay with wide eyes staring into the darkness, thinking of what she felt was a losing battle, the while she held close to her lips the little miniature of Blake, which always hung from her warm throat.

For Yvonne's nature was not that which changed or forgot, and, above all, it was not the nature which gave up hope. Had it been, she must long ere this have slipped quietly out of Blake's life never to reappear in it.

She met them in the hall as they were ushered in, and the warm clasp which passed between her and Blake told of the pure feeling which existed between them, in spite of the deeper things which were held in leash.

After greeting Blake, she turned to Tinker, and both astonished and caused to blush that usually self-possessed lad by placing her arm over his shoulder and wishing him a happy, happy Christmas.

Pedro was compelled to promenade before her with slow dignity, the while the collar was examined by her critical eyes.

At that moment Graves appeared, and the whole party moved on into the library, where the butler served cocktails for Blake, Graves, and Yvonne, and a syrup for Tinker.

Punctually on the minute they went in to dinner. The meal itself was not unlike any other Christmas Eve feast among intimate friends, though perhaps the undoubted force of the individuality of Blake and Yvonne lent an element to the occasion which was lacking in the average gathering.

Grave, sober, and almost curt in his profession, Blake was an admirable dinner companion. His repartee was pointed and brilliant, his fund of small talk inexhaustible, his change of subject sparkling, and as finished as the rapid play of a rapier.

Yvonne was particularly dazzling on this night. She was dressed in a delicate shade of green, with the unmistakable stamp of Paris about it, from the low-cut neck of which her white throat rose like a column of alabaster.

Her bronze-gold hair was dressed low on her head, and fashioned in heavy coils held together by two jewelled clasps. A thin gold chain about her neck guarded a great emerald, which gleamed startlingly deep against her white skin, and on her left hand she wore one ring—an emerald solitaire.

The big stone suspended from the chain at her throat had been Blake's gift to her in the stormy past, and a thin platinum chain, which disappeared beneath her corsage, was mute evidence of the invisible miniature from which she was never parted.

Course after course appeared, and was taken away. As a seasonable banquet it was a huge success, as a product of the culinary art it was a masterpiece.

When the servants had withdrawn, and the decanter was being eyed by Graves with a longing gaze, Yvonne rose and got a small gold cigarette-case filled with her own special brand of Russian cigarettes.

Blake accepted the case Graves pushed over, and for a short space of time they smoked and chatted quietly. Then Graves got to his feet and suggested that Tinker should play him a hundred up in the billiard-room. The lad jumped up with alacrity, and they passed out, leaving Blake and Yvonne alone.

For almost five minutes silence reigned between them; then Yvonne spoke.

"I have been wondering if you would be able to find the time to go for a very short cruise in the Fleur-de-Lys as far as Tunis and back," she said, with a tentative look at Blake.

"It is most awfully kind of you to invite me," answered Blake, warmly, "and I assure you I should like nothing better. If you had asked me last night, or even this morning, I think I should have said 'Yes' without hesitation; but since then I have accepted two commissions which promise to take all that time and resources I have."

"Are they of such a nature that they cannot be put off?"

"I am sorry to say they are. One of them is of a particularly urgent description."

"I am sorry. My uncle and I would have enjoyed having you and Tinker immensely."

"You will go yourself in any event, I presume?" remarked Blake.

Yvonne shrugged her white shoulders.

"It is indefinite as yet. This rain and snow are depressing, and I thought a change would be pleasant."

"I have been racking my brains over something for the past two hours," went on Blake, "and it has just occurred to me that perhaps you might help me out. It would not interfere with your proposed trip, but if you consented, I should like to keep in touch with you, in order to let you know if I needed your help."

"I should be only too delighted," answered Yvonne quickly. "What is the nature of it?"

"It is a case where I may need the presence of a woman in order to look after a young girl. The whole thing rests on whether I am successful or unsuccessful in my quest."

"If that is the case, then I am sure you will need me," said Yvonne softly.

"I am afraid you entertain too high an opinion of my abilities," laughed Blake, with a faint tinge of embarrassment.

"That is not very flattering to my own poor accomplishments," she smiled, with a reminiscent look in her eyes.

"Oh, I didn't mean it that way!" protested Blake. "But to return to the subject of which we were speaking, mademoiselle. Perhaps you would care to hear the facts, since you may be called upon to join in the affair."

"I should be very proud of the confidence."

"I suppose in reading the papers you have noticed the announcement of an exceptionally large reward in the 'Personal Columns'?"

"Fifty thousand, isn't it?"

"Yes."

"Oh, yes, I have seen it for several days running. The description follows of a young girl who is missing. It occurred to me as I read it that she must belong to a wealthy family. I put it down to an elopement with an undesirable suitor."

"That is the explanation which would naturally strike one," responded Blake. "It happens, however, that such is not the case. She has been missing for a matter of two weeks, but only to-day was the matter placed in my hands. It is on account of the great lapse of time that I feel dubious regarding the success of my investigations. But if you care to hear the facts, I will relate them. Needless to say, it is a case for the observance of strict secrecy."

Yvonne lighted a fresh cigarette, and leaned forward, her eyes resting on Blake's.

"Whether or not I can be of assistance in the matter, you know I will respect your confidence."

Blake lighted a cigar, and puffed for a few moments in silence. Then he began.

First he dealt with the visit of the duchess that afternoon, and with the very distinct signs of suffering she evinced. From that he went to the kernel of the subject, and related in detail all she had told him. After that he spoke of the startling coincidence of his sketch of Wu Ling with Dr. Li-Fuang, and of the suspicions such a coincidence had roused in his mind.

Yvonne knew only too well the calibre of Wu Ling, for she had been of no small help to Blake at the time Wu Ling had abducted John Strang, the American multi-millionaire, and she herself had suffered at the hands of the prince. Consequently, she followed Blake's every word with an added interest, and when he finished her lids drooped over her eyes in concentration.

"It is your idea, then, that the daughter of the Duchess of Carrisbrooke has fallen into the hands of Wu Ling?"

"I wouldn't go as far as to say that," responded Blake. "At the same time, it strikes me that it is the girl herself who is wanted. No organisation or individual to whom she was simply worth the price of a human being would be able to resist the enormous reward offered. Of course, Wu Ling's likeness to Dr. Li-Fuang, and his possible identity with that individual, is little to build on at present.

"Most Chinamen look alike to the inexperienced European, as do Europeans to the untravelled Celestial, and it is just possible a certain similarity in the features of Wu Ling to those of Dr. Li-Fuang may have caused the duchess to think it was the doctor. I include those points in my deduction, but the whole structure is of the most unreliable nature so far."

"I judged from what you said that you will go on to Cardiff?"

"Yes. It happens that another case upon which I have entered will take me there and probably to Liverpool as well. Oddly enough it also deals with the Chinese, and even before I had heard the story of the duchess I had decided to go to those places. In any event the beginning of the trail lies in Cardiff.

"If the latter is the case it is more than likely that one of the numerous Chinese secret societies, or 'tongs' has been used as the instrument for her capture and to send her out of the country. They have many devious and secret ways, and who knows, the two roads, apparently so widely divergent, may lead to the same spot in the investigation."

"When will you leave?"

"I have an appointment at ten to-morrow with Kennedy, the American Secret Service man, who has sought my assistance.

"After I have discussed the details with him, I may decide to go on to Cardiff in the afternoon. I shall leave in any event not later than the following morning. Too much valuable time has already been lost. So you see, mademoiselle, why I may need your assistance.

"Into whatsoever hands the Lady Sybil has fallen, she will be in a state of collapse, and will need a cool, sympathetic friend of her own sex to tide her over the reaction. Her own mother would be the worst person in the world for the case, for she would dwell on what had occurred, and that would be bad. Now, can I count on you?"

"You know you can, Mr. Blake," answered Yvonne quickly, "No matter where I am, or what I am doing, I will drop anything, and come out at once as soon as I hear from you. It makes no difference where you wish me to go, or what you wish me to do, I am ready."

"Thank you very much indeed," said Blake, holding out his hand. "I knew I could depend on you."

Yvonne looked at him with a hint of pleading in her eyes.

"Won't you let me help you, anyway? You know my feelings regarding these vampires who cause so much misery to my sex. In order to overcome them and sweep them out of existence one cannot overlook the bald facts or wear gloves in one's treatment of them. I should do everything you said, and perhaps I, as a woman, could discover some of the channels along which so many young girls disappear, in many cases to be kidnapped abroad and married against their wills to wealthy foreigners, where a man, no matter how clever he might be, would fail. Who knows this case might be the means of uncovering a gigantic system."

Blake shook his head and smiled.

"I am sorry, mademoiselle, but I cannot permit it. I have no misgivings as to the thoroughness with which you would do your work, and I would more than back your brains against those of the people we are after; but such a thing as you suggest is fraught with too much danger to you. You might fall into their clutches yourself, and—well, mademoiselle, I—I—"

And for once in his life Blake was at a loss for something to say.

Yvonne's heart contracted with a wild, exquisite pain as Blake's halting words told her that her disappearance would mean a big thing to him, and her eyes grew very soft.

All unconsciously, Blake's reasons for not accepting the offer of her services had started a vague train of thought in Yvonne's mind, and had he only dreamed what it was he would then and there have exacted her solemn promise not to participate in the affair until he sent for her.

Unfortunately, he had no idea of this, and so a tiny idea was formed in Yvonne's mind which was to lead her into the jaws of the System, and to show her the hideous depths of misery which it caused. The same idea was to send Blake into an agony of self-reproach that he had not exacted the promise, and a deadly fear for the safety of the wilful, quixotic girl, who held a bigger place in his affections than he would acknowledge even to himself.

The silence which had fallen upon them was broken by the entrance of Graves and the jubilant Tinker, who had beaten the older man in three straight games.

"Tinker simply played rings around me," grumbled Graves, lighting a cigarette. "I couldn't seem to hit a ball."

"I am seriously considering giving up detective work, and becoming a billiard professional," said Tinker, with mock seriousness. "I will take on Gray first."

"You will, eh?" smiled Blake. "Well, just to take you down a peg, young man, I will give you twenty and play a hundred up."

"I wish I had kept quiet now," grinned the lad. "But come on, guv'nor—I'll take you on."

They all moved back to the billiard-room, where Graves proceeded to make a book with Yvonne on the result. She championed Blake, and Graves was highly pleased, for certainly Tinker had been in great form. But what a sad surprise was in store for the lad and his backer!

From the minute he picked up the cue Blake settled down to business, and it looked as though Tinker was not even going to have a shot. Using a break off the red as his play, Blake engineered the balls up to the top of the table. With them in that position he began to pot from the break into the side pocket, causing the red to cushion about until it struck the lower end of the table and rolled back—to stop within half an inch of where it had lain before.

Yvonne and Graves looked on with keen enjoyment while Blake piled up a great lead. Poor Tinker was entirely out of it.

It was pretty work, and, moreover, not easy. Blake, however, played with deliberation and coolness, not hurrying his shot, and putting exactly the proper force into his stroke. It was a walk over for him from the start, and although Tinker played well when he did get a chance, Blake had chalked up too much against him.

It would be unfair to give the score the lad made, but had he really needed any taking down it was certainly sufficient to give it to him. He did not, however, and took his beating with a cheerful grin.

"I might stand a chance with you if you used one hand," he said ruefully, as he put away his cue.

"My lad, you played very badly," said Blake magnanimously. "Before you take on Gray you want to learn that one off the red."

Then he turned to Mademoiselle Yvonne.

"And now, mademoiselle, I think we will be going. It was awfully kind of you to invite us out of our cave, and I assure you we have more than enjoyed it."

They moved back into the hall, where Tinker and Blake donned their coats. Just as they did so the door-bell rang. It proved to be the chauffeur, who had returned for them, and while Yvonne was speaking with him at the door Blake seized the opportunity to slip back into the library and lay a package on the table.

It was his Christmas present to Yvonne.

Then they departed for Baker Street, though it had required stern measures to dislodge Pedro from his place in front of the fire in the library. And as the powerful car picked its way along the wet streets

44

through which the Christmas crowds still thronged, how little did Blake dream of the decision and move Yvonne was to make before the night was over.

Back in her house Yvonne had wandered into the library, and there discovered the package Blake had left. She unwrapped it at once, and, as her eyes fell on what it contained, an involuntary cry of pleasure broke from her lips.

It was a perfect sphere of pure jade in an exquisite blending of green and pink and lavender shading to pearl. Every inch of its surface was decorated with a series of carvings portraying the descent to earth of the first "Son of Heaven" (the name given to the Chinese emperors) and His supposed formation of the great empire for His chosen people. As an example of ancient workmanship it represented months of the most skilled labour; as an objet d'art its value must have been enormous.

Yvonne knew Blake had picked up several splendid specimens of jade on his last trip to China, and judged the sphere before her to be one of them; but not until she read the note which accompanied it did she know that the piece before her was supposed to have been handed from the first "Son of Heaven" to His successor, and so on to each new emperor through all the untold ages of that mysterious country until it had reached the last ruler of the Ming Dynasty—that line which fell before the conquering Manchus just over two hundred and fifty years ago.

And by the same token it is worthy of note that it was at the same time the "pig-tail" first made its appearance in China, being the form of headdress of the Manchus and imposed by them on the conquered Chinese.

With the last Emperor of the Ming Dynasty the Sacred Sphere of jade disappeared. Many wild tales regarding its fate were spread abroad.

Some said the fleeing "Son of Heaven" had cast it in the Lake of the Three Moons before the Manchu entered the city. The lake was emptied, and though many skeletons of bygone victims were found, there was no sign of the Sphere.

Others said that the High Mandarin had secreted it in order to present it to the Ming Emperor when he should return to the throne. He lost his head over it, but if he knew where the Sphere was he did not speak.

Again it was said that the first "Son of Heaven" had stretched down His hand from above and had snatched it away in anger that the Manchu should rule, and that now it reposed with him. Be that as it may, the Sphere was never found, and in the course of time, when all hope of its recovery was given up, the latter story became the one most generally accepted. And now after all these ages it had come to light.

In his rather bulky letter regarding it Blake mentioned all these facts, and added:

"I need not tell you, mademoiselle, that did the Chinese know of its existence each one would strain his every nerve in order to recover it. Above all, would Prince Wu Ling do so; for, remember, he is the only royal descendant of the ancient Ming Dynasty, and looks upon the later Manchu as an upstart and usurper, though in reality he himself is Manchu of an older generation.

"With the Sacred Sphere in his possession he would become even more powerful than at present. The sight of it would rally every Celestial in the country to his banner, and, in their excited fanaticism, they would sweep over the earth with all their millions in a flood no human dam could withstand. For that reason you will see the necessity for keeping its presence in your collection—to which I hope it will add an interest—a profound secret."

When she had read and re-read Blake's letter Yvonne excitedly called to her uncle, who was lazily knocking the balls about on the billiard-table. He came through at once and examined the Sphere with interest, the while Yvonne explained its history, and added for his benefit Blake's caution.

"What will you do with it?" he asked, when he had completed his examination of the cycle of pictures which formed the story on the Sphere.

Yvonne shrugged.

"Since Mr. Blake has so definitely expressed the need for secrecy regarding my possession of it I can only act accordingly. It is a great temptation to put it in the case with my other jades, but the very fact that he thought me worthy of receiving such a gift makes it incumbent upon me to prevent any publicity regarding it. It is not large, and since that is so I think I shall keep it where I keep the thing I value most highly."

Graves smiled. "And that, I imagine, is the invisible something which hangs from the chain about your neck."

"Exactly," answered Yvonne coolly. "I shall put it in a chamois bag this very night and attach it."

She took it in her hand as she spoke and turned towards the door.

"You will not be going to bed for some time, I suppose?" she said, pausing and looking back over her shoulder.

"No. I shall be smoking and reading for at least an hour yet. Why?"

"It is just possible I may be down again. I have some thinking to do."

"Good heavens, you are not planning another coup, are you, Yvonne?"

"If I am it is not of the nature you think," she laughed. "If I am not down again within an hour you will know I have retired."

With that she was gone, and, with a shrug, the luxury-loving Graves settled down in an easy-chair before the fire and picked up a magazine.

"Heaven knows what is running in her mind," he muttered, as he lighted a cigarette. "I wonder if it has emanated from any remark of Blake's. They seemed to be talking very earnestly together after dinner. Heigho! I suppose I shall be dragged out again to go rampaging half over the globe and be kept busy dodging the law."

On reaching her room Yvonne closed and locked the door, then she crossed quickly to a small easy-chair which stood before a cheerful open fire. Sinking into it she propped her elbows on her knees and sank her chin in the cupped palms of her hands.

The ticking of the little gold clock on the mantel was the only sound which broke the silence of the next half hour. At the end of that time she stirred and lifted her head. As she did so her eyes rested on the Sphere, which she still clutched tightly.

"Yes," she murmured softly, though her eyes held the faintest touch of weariness in them, "I will do it—for him. He does care what becomes of me, and I—I will prove to him what I can and will do."

With that she rose abruptly and approached the dressing-table. Pulling out a drawer she took out a small morocco jewel-case. Opening this she searched about until she found a small chamois bag containing a diamond-studded watch. The watch she returned to the jewel-case, after which she placed the Sphere in the chamois pocket.

It fitted perfectly, and it was not long before her nimble fingers had drawn out the miniature and fastened the bag on the chain beside it. That done she pushed them both back beneath her corsage and passed out of the room.

Graves was still sitting in his comfortable position before the library fire when Yvonne entered.

"So you have decided," he said, laying down his magazine.

She nodded, and drew up a chair beside him. "Yes, uncle, I have. I am sorry to spoil the trip we had planned to take, but after carefully thinking the matter over I have decided to leave for Cardiff to-night."

"Leave for Cardiff to-night!" echoed Graves, in astonishment. "What on earth for?"

"Listen, and I will tell you."

Then Yvonne began, and told him briefly what Blake had told her, though she kept all names to herself.

"He would not say so," she went on, "but I know that the assistance of a woman in this affair would be of great value to him. On thinking the matter over, however, I have struck what is in my opinion the best mode of procedure."

"And that is?"

"To reproduce as far as is possible the exact outrage which was perpetrated upon the girl, who is missing."

"I don't think I follow you."

"It is very simple. I shall put myself in a position where, if they so desire, the System will have every opportunity of kidnapping me."

"But, good heavens, Yvonne, that is madness! You put yourself in deadly peril. I refuse utterly to countenance any such idea."

"I have quite made up my mind, uncle, and I think my own brains will carry me through any immediate danger. The ultimate success of the move will depend upon the way in which you carry out what you have to do, and whether Mr. Blake succeeds in following up the lead I give. If you both fail, of course, I shall find myself in an unenviable position. But you must not fail—he will not fail."

"Perhaps you will deign to be a little more explicit," said Graves sarcastically.

"I will," she replied imperturbably. "While I am changing you will ring up the garage and have Alec bring around the big motor. He can drive, and we will get away by midnight for Cardiff.

"To-morrow we shall have an opportunity to spy out the land, and to-morrow night I shall begin to put into operation the plan I have thought out. If it fails, then I shall try the next and the next night until I succeed or see that it is useless."

"A nice way to spend Christmas Day," grumbled Graves.

"For the purpose I have in mind no day could be better," she replied, rising. "I shall be down in less than half an hour, so please get Alec on the 'phone at once."

While Yvonne hurried away to change and pack what she desired Graves proceeded to do her bidding. Punctually at the end of half an hour she was down again, carrying a small handbag.

She found her uncle eyeing the cosy fire regretfully, and had Yvonne only dreamed in the slightest degree what she was to go through before she again stood in that comfortable room even her intrepid soul would have quailed.

But it is the mercy of Nature that, in most all the big things of life, we are ignorant of the pitfalls and dangers surrounding them. Were it otherwise, man would have scratched the elate of achievement far less deeply than he has.

A few minutes later Alec arrived. He was too inured to the sudden whims of his mistress to show any surprise at the unusual summons, and had Yvonne calmly announced that she intended leaving for the middle of the Sahara, it is a safe bet that Alee would have made his preparations without the quiver of an eyelash.

For much of the success of Yvonne's daring coups in the past was due to the unswerving loyalty and frank worship of every member of her famous "circle."

Yvonne led the way to the waiting motor, and when most of London was wrapped in sleep— the adults with pleasant dreams of the restful morrow and the children with rosy mind pictures of the treat in store for them—the rhythmic hum of the engine purred a lullaby as the big car started on its long journey.

Yvonne curled herself up in the corner of the tonneau, and almost before the last lights of London had been left behind she was fast asleep. Graves smoked for some time in silence, then he, too, succumbed to the song of the engine, and only Alec remained awake, sitting motionless over his wheel, his goggled eyes fixed rigidly on the dark road ahead.

For all the world he might have been some relentless gargoyle steering a thundering Juggernaut through the wet mystery of the night.

From the time they left London until they made the outskirts of

Cardiff, the engine never changed the tone of its song, up hill and down hill, through muddy, narrow lanes and along lonely level stretches it had gone without a change of gear.

As they entered the first of the streets of that coal-begrimed city, however, Alec slowed down and turned his head the barest trifle.

"Where shall I drive, mademoiselle?"

His voice awoke Yvonne, and when he had repeated his question, she murmured sleepily:

"The Hotel North."

Through the silent streets they sped, past long lines of small tenements until they reached the better quarter; then came the technical schools, the museum, the public library, and, finally the Hotel North. There Yvonne and Graves alighted, their luggage being taken in by a yawning night porter.

Alec departed to put the car in the garage, and the others went at once to their rooms. It was still dark, and making an appointment to meet for lunch at twelve, Yvonne and Graves retired.

At that very moment Tinker and Blake were fast asleep at Baker Street, all unaware of the distance which Yvonne had put between herself and them since they had left Queen Anne's Gate the previous evening.

It was certainly a strange way in which Yvonne spent that Christmas afternoon. Immediately after lunch she had the car brought round, and before entering it, took care to heavily veil her features. She directed Alec to drive slowly through the streets by the docks where the Chinese quarter is situated, and certainly not even the dingy purlieu of Limehouse exceed in sinister suggestion the dock dens of Cardiff.

Like Liverpool, New York, Melbourne, and all seaport towns, it attracts to its meaner districts a horde of the lowest vampires in human form, spawn of vampires before them, and progenitors of other vampires to come.

Night born and night bred, their days are spent in idleness waiting for the hours of darkness, when their nefarious trades can be carried on and their pockets profit accordingly.

Since its marvellous leap into the position of a great point of export and the prosperity given to it by the great South Wales coal mines which feed it, Cardiff has reached a rank of greatness in its business and a level of depravity in its dens.

There, the sailor arriving from a long voyage and with money in his pocket, falls an easy prey to the sharks which are ever on his track, but in this it is no better, no worse, than other placed of a similar nature.

But large or small, there is something in the Chinese atmosphere of such a place which deepens the sinister meaning of its purpose and creates an abyss of mysterious retreats into which many men and women disappear, never to come to the surface.

And it was into this type of nest which Yvonne went that afternoon.

Though her veil was heavy, enough to conceal her features, it was not too heavy to prevent her keen eyes from photographing on the retina of her mind an accurate impression of the district and the plan of its streets.

For two solid hours the motor turned up one street and down another; then Yvonne signified her wish to return to the hotel.

Over a cup of tea in the sitting-room of her suite, Yvonne gave Graves his final instructions.

"I shall leave here at half-past seven," she said. "I want you to follow me at a discreet distance. Be sure and keep far enough behind to attract no attention. It will be necessary for you to put on a rough suit, and as far as possible assume the appearance of a sailor ashore for Christmas Day. That will guard against suspicion being aroused. Have Alec do the same, and take him with you.

"As for me, I have brought a disguise. It will give me the appearance of a girl from the country, and I fancy I can carry off the part. Of course, nothing may happen at all, but one never knows. If any of the agents of the System are about, they are sure to remark my appearance in that district alone, and the unsophisticated nature of my appearance will lead them to think that I am a country girl in Cardiff for the day, who has lost her way—which is what I desire. If that does occur, I shall then look for some move on their part.

"It will have to be strategy, for I shall not give them the opportunity to take me by force. That is why I shall stick to the more frequented thoroughfares. I am hoping that one of them will approach me, and inquire if I have lost my way. When I say 'Yes,' they are bound to offer to show me how to go, and if they are of the System, that way will be into one of the retreats where they will keep me.

"That is where you and Alec come in. Do nothing if such a thing occurs; but follow cautiously, and watch where I am taken. From that moment it will be necessary for one of you to remain on watch every moment. They may keep me a day, they may keep me a week; but I fancy it will not be longer than that. It is their policy to get their captives out of the country as soon as possible. I shall probably be taken away with a batch of others, and it is bound to be at night.

"I have wired to Captain Vaughan at Plymouth to steam around here, at once with the Fleur-de- Lys. As I came in this afternoon I received an answer saying he had left. He should be here to-night. Tell him what I have done, and watch carefully to which ship I am taken. Do nothing even then, but watch for her departure.

"By that time Mr. Blake should be here. Tell him all the facts, and have him join you. As soon as the ship on which I am taken departs, follow in the yacht. Then you must do the rest yourselves.

"It is certain that no harm will come to me until I reach my destination, wherever that may be. But you must move before then. I would suggest training the bow gun of the Fleur-de-Lys on her after she got to sea, and boarding her; but, of course, Mr. Blake may prefer to follow on in the yacht and make no move until she reaches port. That I leave to you.

"Only one thing, uncle, let me impress upon you. The whole success of my plan depends upon the ability of you and Alec to make sure first of the retreat to which I am taken, and, secondly, of the ship by which I shall be taken out of the country."

"I said back in London, and I say now, Yvonne, that the whole plan is madness. You will, however, do as you have made up your mind to do, and that being so, I can only second your efforts to the best of my ability. You may rest assured that both I and Alec will be on the job each minute and watch every move."

"I know you will," answered Yvonne. "Only" and as she spoke there was a little catch in her voice—"it would be terrible if you missed me. And now I shall get ready. You had better do the same."

At half-past seven that evening, when the Christmas festivities were at their height all over the city Yvonne, dressed as a demure country girl, made her way from the hotel and turned in the direction leading to the congested, odious district by the docks.

And as she walked along she murmured softly:

"It is for him! Oh, if I can only succeed! But—but if I fail!"

Rymer writes his treatise "On the Emanations of Radium in Relation to their Action on Cancer, and the Curative Power Thereof."

AMONGST all the vessels which were in the Port of Cardiff for over Christmas there was one moored at a lonely quay in the shadow of a great coal shed, which had as captain, mate, and crew as choice a collection of seaport scrapings as one could find in a world tour. Her name was Eastern Queen.

She was a brigantine of ancient build, and her patched sails from the mizzen sail forward to the living jib and aloft to her topgallant sails told of a skimpy owner or a captain who stuffed his expense sheets.

It happened that in the present instance the former was the case, for Captain Jonas Pettigrew was both master and owner, and not a penny did he spend on the ship, which for many years had given him a nefarious living, beyond absolute necessaries.

Not that he hadn't the money. He had plenty, for he was one of the few individuals who had reduced the game of illegal gain to a fine art, and, unlike most of his ilk, hoarded his money. Had Jonas Pettigrew lived two hundred years ago, he would have made a name for himself as a contemporary of Morgan, Kidd, and Black Peter of Spanish Main fame. But he was by no means discouraged at this unfortunate delay in his entry into this world.

Ever since the Eastern Queen had come into his possession twenty years before, by the simple expedient of knocking her captain and owner overboard whilst trading among the South Sea Islands, Captain Jo had done many things and had sailed on many strange cruises.

Of recent years he had been occupied in the profitable pursuit of smuggling arms into Morocco, and it was only during the past six months that he had taken on a new and even more profitable lay.

This was, so he deemed, a cinch, for it consisted of leading human cargo aboard at Cardiff, and sailing with it to different ports, but mostly to Canada.

As mate he had a man whom he had picked up years ago in Sydney, and a worthy understudy of his chief. The crew were a mixture of white, black, and yellow, and consisted of the port scrapings of New York, 'Frisco, Shanghai, Sydney, Melbourne, Alexandria, and Heaven knows where else.

The safe delivery of his previous cargo, plus a steady, fair wind, had enabled Captain Jonas Pettigrew to return to Cardiff, presumably from the successful delivery of a cargo of coal in Canada.

Most of the crew had gone ashore on the previous day, and had wasted little time seeking their favourite dens, there to spend the great day in drinking, gambling, or "hitting the pipe," whichever way their fancy took them. Be very sure their ideas of a happy Christmas did not rise above that level of depravity.

Dropped into this world from ancestors of a similar breed, kicked and beaten through a depraved childhood, sent with curses and blows before they grew up to steal a living in any way that offered, they are hardly to be blamed, considering that they knew nothing cleaner or better.

But what a field for education, instead of spending huge sums in trying to convert the Chinese and Moslems who do not wish to be converted.

As long as a man lives steeped in such an atmosphere his moral senses become more and more blunted until anything clean or straight or decent looks to him namby-pamby. And yet, in his heart—and he undoubtedly has some semblance of that organ—he must know that the cheap depravity of the lower levels is a losing game—not only from a moral, but from a physical, a mental and a financial point of view.

The youth who, in a spirit of unwise emulation attempts to fill his pockets by the get-rich-quick method of accumulation, has about as much chance of ultimate success as a snowball has of remaining intact in the middle of the Sahara desert.

And it is because the average well-intentioned individual works only upon the theory of moral downfall that the beginner in the crook game thrusts aside warnings with the disdainful optimism of ignorant and inexperienced youth.

If he understood straight from the shoulder that he was hitting the trail others had hit, and was travelling at an unbelievable pace towards the point where he would become a doddering old fool at forty, a physical mass of repulsion, or the inmate of a six by ten cell, he might begin to see that the game was a poor one from the start.

The odds in draw poker are pretty heavy against the player, but the odds against the punter in the crook game are stupendous.

All the crew had not gone ashore, however. The cook, a big

negro from Martinique, had remained aboard, preferring the company of a bottle of Jamaica rum in the solitude of his galley rather than the more noisy—and expensive-hilarity of the dens.

Besides him, one of the sailors was loafing about the fo'castle, preferring to wait until the hours of darkness before venturing ashore and inevitably returning before daybreak.

The captain and mate were also aboard, but beyond that delightful quartette, the ship was deserted.

Had any of the others looked in upon the solitary sailor in the fo'castle during the afternoon, they would have found him occupied by an odd form of recreation for a member of the crew of the Eastern Queen.

He was sitting against the end of a bulkhead near the door, which was half open in order to permit some light to enter the fo'castle. Though it was a cold, raw December day outside, he apparently felt it not, for he betrayed no sign.

Between his teeth was the stem of an old pipe, and rising from the bowl was the blue smoke spiral of heavy blackjack. On his knees rested a small book of red leather, in which he was writing rapidly; and therein lay the wonder ol his occupation, for had one examined the written words closely, it would have been seen that they were of a strangely technical nature, and had the examination been extended to include all that had been written, one would have been astonished to discover that it was the partially completed manuscript of a profound treatise "On the Emanations of Radium in Relation to their Action on Cancer, and the Curative Power Thereof."

It was a technical effort which would add lustre to the name of the most prominent scientist, but nothing more incongruous could well be found than such a work being conceived and written by a rough, bearded sailor in the filthy fo'castle of one of the most disreputable ships afloat.

But so it was, and had some of the aforesaid scientists read the work, they would have shaken their heads, and said it was strangely like the language of that once famous surgeon, Dr. Huxton Rymer, who had suddenly dropped out of the exalted position in his profession which he once held, and had disappeared from the ken of his old associates. And, strangest of all, they would have been right, for it was Rymer, and no other.

Even the black scrubby beard of several weeks' growth failed to hide the heavy sweep of the powerful jaw; though cut and bruised and stained, the fingers still had the long, sensitive appearance which was an index to the man's nervous capacity with the knife; the face still possessed the marks of past refinement, though the eyes were beginning to have a brooding look which in the past a certain vein of optimism had kept at bay. How he came to be an ordinary seaman aboard the Eastern Queen is very soon told.

Some time previously Rymer had been in a fair way to clean up a big haul in Ecuador, and, in fact, had already clinched a hundred thousand pounds before Sexton Blake had stepped in and upset his nicely-planned little coup.

Unfortunately for Rymer, this interference on Blake's part plus the vengeance of a certain Indian whom he had betrayed, had made Ecuador too hot to hold him, and had necessitated his seeking a more salubrious climate.

Through Blake's magnanimity, prompted by the detective's own desire to keep certain diplomatic occurrences a secret from the general public, there had been no police information passed against Rymer, and, as a consequence, he found in New York the salubrious atmosphere of which he was in search.

There he got hold of the money which he had salted away, and for a time spared nothing in the gratifying of the most extravagant taste. Even a hundred thousand can be spent in time if nothing is being added to it, and when Rymer began hitting the faro table, it began to have some big holes made in it. A few weeks of this, and he awoke one morning to find his balance consisted of only ten thousand.

That day he drew every penny, and in the evening sought the gambling rooms. In a spirit of reckless bravado, he put the whole lot on the ace to win.

It lost, and on this one turn of the cards departed Rymer's hopes of recouping himself. Then he had wandered out, and with the loose notes which he found about his clothes, plus a hundred dollars which the house had loaned him on leaving, he made for the east side, and began to steep himself in spirits.

At the end of a week he woke up to find himself lying on a couch in the back room of some dingy den, and a conversation which he had overheard there had resulted in his offering his services to the speakers.

They turned out to be Captain Jonas Pettigrew and the mate of the Eastern Queen, and since then Rymer had been one of the most exemplary seamen aboard. A couple of fights in the fo'castle had achieved his standing there, and now none bothered him. That was just previous to the last voyage of the Eastern Queen from Cardiff.

When the dying light made it impossible for Rymer to follow the fine lines, he closed the book with a heavy sigh, and placed it carefully in the inside pocket of his waistcoat.

At times the true scientific nature of the man predominated, and it was during those moments that an outlet of some kind was necessary—an outlet which he found in the compilation of his treatise. No sooner had he put the book away, however, than the scientist gave place to the other element in him.

Rising softly to his feet, he took a careful look through the open door along the deserted deck; then he once more thrust his hand in his pocket.

It emerged, clutching the folded clipping from a newspaper which he carefully spread out. Only one complete announcement had escaped the rough cutting, and this he proceeded to read.

It was headed:

"FIFTY THOUSAND POUNDS REWARD OFFERED.

"The above reward will be paid, and no questions asked, for information leading to the immediate recovery of a young lady of the following description:

"About five feet six inches in height, fair hair and complexion, fine, regular features, blue eyes, a tiny mole under the left ear, and a barely perceptible dimple in the centre of the chin.

"At the time of her disappearance she was dressed in an evening gown of pale pink, was wearing black satin pumps, and over her gown a heavy fur coat of grey squirrel.

"Disappeared from Cardiff on the evening of the eleventh. All communications respecting the above to be addressed to Crick, Palmer & Martin, Solicitors, London and Liverpool. Strict secrecy guaranteed under all conditions."

When he had read it and re-read it, Rymer folded up the paper and thrust it back in his pocket then he leaned against the bulkhead, and smoked thoughtfully.

"We left here two months ago," he muttered, "so there was no chance of her being in the cargo we took. Anyway, although I didn't get a squint at the Chinks we had, I would have heard something about it if there had been a woman aboard. Of course, since the Chinese, the Japs, the Turks and that breed don't dare come on and publicly marry English girls, they manage to get them as wives just the same, and with all due respect to Captain Jonas Pettigrew, I imagine he has been the means of bringing 'married bliss' (?) to more than one Celestial.

"The point is, from what den here was she taken, and by what route was she got out of the country? I have been in this cursed ship long enough to discover that there are many underground routes having their genesis in Cardiff; but what I can't figure out is whether she was taken East or by way of America. If I could only discover that, I should be a long way on my investigations.

"The very fact that such a reward has been offered, and is still being offered, proves that she comes from a high family, and that she must be intended as the wife of some mighty exalted foreigner who knew his chances of receiving her consent to marry him in the ordinary way were jolly remote.

"But that fifty thousand gets my eye. If I can put my fingers on it, I will do so, and to blazes with Captain Jonas Pettigrew and his cursed ship! My first move is to hang about the dens, and see if I can find out what ships of this nature have left Cardiff during the past two weeks; then, with that infonnation, I can perhaps trace which den supplied her cargo, and then drop on what I want. This is too big a thing to let slip through my fingers."

At that moment Captain Jonas Pettigrew himself came along the deck, and thrust his bearded face through the open doorway.

"When are you going ashore for your leave?" he asked, in a strangely mild tone.

He did not know to this day just what Rymer may have overheard in the New York joint, and, in addition to that, there was an intangible something about his newest recruit which caused him to use a less snarling tone than to his other seamen.

Rymer eyed him coolly.

"I had intended leaving the ship about seven, Captain Pettigrew. Have you any particular reason for asking?"

"Yes. If you want to put in much time, you had better leave earlier. We take on a cargo to-night, and, as the tide serves, we will get down channel at daybreak. The people ashore want to take advantage of the fact that it is Christmas night. A less strict watch will be kept."

Rymer was keenly disappointed to hear that they were sailing so soon, for he had little hopes of being able to complete his investigations in one evening. It would have bothered him not a whit to desert the ship, did such a move suit his purpose, but he felt that while aboard the Eastern Queen he was, in a way, in direct touch with the System he was endeavouring to fathom, and that there, if any place, he would find what he sought.

Even if he failed to track the missing girl and swell his slender resources by the addition of the magnificent reward, he might drop on to something which would serve as a lever for causing the System to disgorge some of its ill-gotten gains. Not for nothing was Dr. Huxton Rymer content to remain an ordinary seaman. These reasons caused him to curb any disappointment he felt.

"All right, captain," he said briefly. "I have very little to do. I shall be aboard again before we sail."

"Very well. The mate and I are going ashore to beat up the crew. I suppose the blinking loafers are all drunk."

With that the bearded face withdrew, and his heels sounded heavily as he stamped back along the deck. Once he had gone, Rymer lost no time in preparing to go ashore.

In less than five minutes he had donned a heavy coat, stuck a soft slouch hat on his head, and drawn on a pair of gloves. This done, he opened the sea-chest under his bunk, and took out an automatic revolver, which he dropped in the outside pocket of his overcoat. Then he kicked open the fo'castle door, and made his way along the deck and over the side to the quay.

For several minutes he walked through a maze of narrow, silent streets lined with warehouses. Turning out of these, he came to a saloon on a corner which stood as the outpost to the illuminated district beyond. Along this street went Rymer until he came to a narrow side street, turning off to the right. A few yards up he paused, and knocked at a door.

It opened almost at once to admit him, and he found himself in a low-ceiled room containing a bar against the opposite wall. Against the other walls were rude benches, upon which sat a conglomeration of seamen representing almost every nationality imaginable.

The air was heavy with the fumes of beer, spirits, and tobacco, and a babel of talk ascended from all sides. The bar-tender was a Chinaman. It was the den where Rymer hoped to discover the names of any likely ships which had sailed within the past two weeks.

Strolling across to the bar, he ordered a whisky, and when he had received it, took it to a corner somewhat away from the crowd. Near him was a half-intoxicated seaman from the Eastern Queen, and from his own words Rymer knew this man was posted on most of the inside facts regarding the underground business of the port.

He made no attempt to get into conversation with the fellow, but waited for the other to make the first advance. They were not long in coming. As his bleary eyes recognised Rymer he shifted nearer.

"Hallo, ol' sport!" he said thickly. "Thought you were stayin' aboard."

Rymer smiled genially.

"I thought I would come away for an hour or two," he replied. "Did you know we were sailing at daybreak?"

"Is that right?"

"No doubt about it. The captain told me just before I came ashore."

Then Rymer sank his voice to a confidential pitch.

"He said the people ashore were taking advantage of the fact that it was Christmas night, and intended rushing a cargo aboard to-night."

The other nodded solemnly.

"Yesh," he said, "they think the United States have agents at every port watching for departures, but I don't think sho. I know every bloomin' bend in the game, and I ain't never seen no agents all the years I been mixed up in it. No, I haven't."

Rymer shrugged.

"I suppose they have to be cautious?" he said carelessly.

"Cautious!" snorted the other. "Le' me tell you, my friend, they're a lot of blamed fools, thash wha' they are. I could run five times as many out of thish 'ere port than they do. Yesh, I could."

"Oh, I agree with you there. At the same time, they ship a good many, I guess?"

The other nodded heavily.

"Yesh, a good many, but not ash many ash they could. Why they ain't sent none since the Belle of 'Frisco sailed two weeks ago. The cargo we take will be the first since. Though, min' you, ol' sport, I only tell you this because you're a shipmate."

"Oh, you needn't worry," rejoined Rymer, with a yawn. "Have another drink?"

The inebriated one decided he would, and when it had disappeared, Rymer seized the opportunity of a diversion created by several new arrivals and slipped out.

"Got it first shot," he muttered, as he strode quickly down the street. "I might have guessed it. The Belle of 'Frisco, she is an old steam tramp, and ready to be piled on the rocks. If I remember rightly, she takes the underground cargo to Canada, and transfers it to a boat out of St. John. And it's Sam Loo who is agent. It is a good thing I kept my ears open aboard the old Eastern Queen."

So absorbed was Rymer in his thoughts, that he almost passed the street leading to Sam Loo's place. The necessity for recalling himself to his surroundings caused him to look up, and his brows knit slightly as he saw ahead of him a man whom he knew as an habitue of Sam Loo's, and a girl, who looked as out of place in that district as Rymer in his present garb would look at a Court function.

She was for all the world like a country maiden who had come into the city for Christmas, and in the confusion of its crowds and streets, had lost her way.

Unconsciously, Rymer slowed up in order not to overtake them, though after the first cursory glance, he gave the pair little attention. In that district one saw many queer sights, and certainly it was none of Rymer's business.

The pair ahead continued up the dark street, until Rymer saw the man pause. A second glance showed him that it was exactly in front of Sam Loo's door. Then that which followed happened so quickly, that it was all over in a moment.

The man turned like lightning on his companion and threw an arm about her shoulder. Well, Rymer knew what that meant, for in the hand would be a drug-soaked handkerchief which would soon cause the victim's senses to flee. Any stranger in the district would think it only an inebriated couple; any frequenter of the district would not give it a second glance.

Rymer saw the girl struggle for a few moments; then, as the drug overcame her, she relaxed and sank back in the man's arms. Picking her up as though she were a child, her assailant carried her to a side door leading into Sam Loo's, and disappeared through it. Like a shot Rymer was after him, and before the door clicked to, he was inside.

To his surprise he found himself in a well-furnished room, where Captain Jonas Pettigrew and the mate of the Eastern Queen sat drinking with Sam Loo himself.

The man who had entered before Rymer, was in the very act of laying his burden on a couch. Sam Loo had started to rise, but on seeing Rymer, he sank back with a snarl, for, though like the rest of the crew, Rymer was admitted to the outer rooms, only those on the inside, like Captain Pettigrew and the mate, were admitted to the heart of the den.

Rymer saw that only bluff would carry him through, though certainly the presence of the captain was an asset.

"What you want?" snapped the Chinaman. "You get to blazes out."

Rymer coolly drew out a cigar and lighted it before replying.

"There is no need to get nervous, Sam," he said, quietly. "Captain Pettigrew will tell you I am one of his men, and all right. Moreover, he has appointed me second mate of the Eastern Queen, and so you see, as I rather thought I would find him in here, I am not infringing any rules by coming."

The mate gasped in amazement, and with Sam Loo, turned to hear Rymer's extraordinary statement indignantly denied by the captain. The latter, however, was looking at Rymer.

To tell the truth, he was quite as surprised to hear Rymer say he had been appointed second mate as were the others, but had Sam Loo and the mate followed his gaze, they would have lead in Rymer's eyes an explanation of what followed.

In those compelling eyes, Captain Jonas Pettigrew for the first time saw he had met his master. Therein he read a nameless menace to himself did he deny the truth of Rymer's statement, and, had he any lingering doubts about the wisdom of agreeing with the seaman of whom he had always secretly stood in awe, the suggestive bulge in Rymer's outside coat pocket settled them. He took a big gulp of spirits, then laughed shortly.

"I didn't intend to announce it until we sailed," he said, turning first to Sam Loo and then to the mate, "but it makes no difference. Yes, I have appointed him second mate."

"But he ain't got no papers," exclaimed the mate, incredulously.

"Pardon me, but you are mistaken," put in Rymer. "I have master's papers." (which happened to be the truth, owing to the fact that among the many things collected in a long career, were the papers of a captain who had met a sudden end in Rio, and of whose effects Rymer had mysteriously become possessed).

No sooner did Sam Loo hear the captain's confirmation of Rymer's statement, than his manner changed like magic. He became once more the suave, smiling Celestial, for it paid to stand in with all those who were of such assistance to him in disposing of his peculiar cargoes.

Moreover, a more detailed look at the stranger's face told him there was indeed a man to be reckoned with.

He rose and bowed.

"My congratulations," he said in tolerable English. "We dlink your health in a few moments."

Turning to the captain he added:

"It is, then, all right to discuss matters before him?" Pettigrew, after another furtive glance at Rymer's eyes, nodded.

"Oh, yes. He is one of us now."

"In that case we will go over and see what Jerry has brought," said the Celestial.

The man who had captured the girl had disappeared almost at once on entering, but now reappeared, bringing in tow an old woman, who might have been of any nationality, so wizened and bent and yellow was she. Sam Loo waved them both aside, and the quartette drew close to inspect the unconscious girl.

Before them they saw a young woman with the bloom of health in her cheeks, and the curve of youth in her features. She was dressed simply as any country maid would dress, but even had she been garbed in rags, nothing could have concealed the pure beauty of her face. As Sam Loo saw it he breathed deeply.

"It is fine—fine," he said, betrayed out of his usual Oriental restraint. "His Excellency Fu Kan, Governor of the district of Hamai, has sought a wife for many months. She will do him, and it will be a fitting reward for her. She will become his wife, and the wife of the Governor of Hamai is a personage in China."

"How will you send her?" asked Captain Pettigrew.

All at once Sam Loo became the man of business.

"She might go by the Belle of 'Frisco," he said carelessly, "or by the Eastern Queen, if you care to handle the matter."

"I am quite willing," responded the captain. "And the price?"

"The same as always—one hundred pounds."

"The governor of a district in China will pay many thousands for such a wife," broke in Rymer. "Since by your own words she will become a lady of such station, one hundred pounds is not enough. It is worth five hundred, and five hundred you must pay."

The mate, who was always governed by Captain Pettigrew, said nothing, and strange to say it was to Rymer, and not to the captain, Sam Loo turned to begin the haggling.

To his surprise, Rymer had not named a high price with the intention of coming down, and when he stuck to the original sum without giving a trifle the Celestial, after half an hour of solid argument, spread out his hands in defeat.

"Have it if you will," he said. "It is robbery."

Rymer smiled and sat down, and the avaricious glint in the captain's eye told him he had established himself solidly in the latter's confidence; for the road to Captain Pettigrew's hatred or liking was through his pocket.

The old woman departed with her charge, followed by the man Jerry, and the quartette were left to drink the health of the new mate, which had been postponed.

And even as they raised their glasses were Graves and Alec planted outside watching the house into which the country girl had vanished, for it was Yvonne, and that had been the end to her daring plan.

To become the wife of a Chinese governor!

When the drinks had been disposed of, Captain Pettigrew rose, and the others followed suit.

"What time will you send the cargo aboard?" he asked, turning to Sam Loo.

"It is now nine. They will be at the ship by eleven."

"All right. We will go along and beat up the crew and be there to receive them."

After a few more words, the three seamen departed, leaving Sam Loo to despatch his cargo. This he proceeded to do at once.

Going to an inner room he called to another Celestial. The latter, a short fat individual, appeared at once.

"Have you the full number ready?" asked Sam Loo curtly.

"Yes—forty," replied the other.

"Send only thirty-nine. Keep one back, I care not which. Send them through the underground passage to the next street. Let them start from there one by one at intervals of a minute, and make their way to the dock where the Eastern Queen lies. Have a taxi called and see that it is drawn up in that street. I will take the fortieth to the ship-myself."

The other turned at once to obey, and Sam Loo departed to get ready to take the intended wife of a Chinese governor to the ship which would start her on her long journey.

Captain Jonas Pettigrew drew up as soon as he reached the street outside Sam Loo's joint. Turning to the mate he said:

"Make tracks into Sam's front bar, Kelly, and dig up any of the crew who are there then hunt out the rest, and see that the drunken dogs get aboard in time. We will go along and get ready for the cargo."

As the mate swung and made off, Pettigrew turned to Rymer.

"You come along to the ship with me. You and I have one or two things to talk over."

Rymer made no reply, preferring to wait until he reached the Eastern Queen before having any explanation and possibly a row. If the latter became necessary, he wished the solitude of the captain's cabin, where he had no personal doubts about the outcome.

They lumbered along in silence, until the black bulk of the coal-shed on the quay loomed up, then appeared the tall spars of the vessel, looking strangely slender against the cold starlit sky. On going aboard, they discovered the negro cook was the only one there so far, and he was for the once out of commission in the solitude of his galley.

Pettigrew led the way aft, and on reaching the saloon, closed the door which opened into the companion-way.

"Now then, Hutton, or whatever your name is," he said, "perhaps you will favour me with an explanation as to why you have appointed yourself second mate of the Eastern Queen?"

"Why, you said in Sam Loo's that you yourself had done that," replied Rymer coolly, lighting another cigar.

"Cut out the hot air, and get to business," snapped the captain.

Rymer's jaws came together with a click, and he swung sharply:

"Look here, Captain Jonas Pettigrew," he said in low, curt tones. "I happened to overhear a certain conversation of yours in New York, which gave me a fair idea of the business upon which you were engaged. It just happened that I was looking for an opening where the profits would be rather more than the exact return for work done. If I had been a stool pigeon or a spy, I could have greened your game on the first call of the cards. I didn't, but I kept my eyes and ears open, and I know the ropes now.

"You know, as sure as you stand there, that I am no ordinary seaman, nor would I remain one for long. With me, it is a case of 'fifty fifty' at least, and that is why I have become your second mate. Use me square and you will find I will do the same by you. When I get tired of the Eastern Queen and her affairs, I will slip away quietly, and no one will ever be the wiser from anything I know. If you allow me a hand in the game, you will find your returns bigger, as they were tonight in Sam Loo's.

"Put me in charge of your cargoes; let me into the inside know of this system, and it will pay you. Now which is it to be, peace or war? And before you answer, let me tell you I am a bad enemy for any man to have."

Pettigrew bit the end off a cigar.

"I guess you have slipped one over on me this time," he grunted, "But let it be peace. You remain second mate."

"And you put me wise to the inside workings of the game?" persisted Rymer.

"Sure. To-morrow we will talk."

Rymer breathed a sigh of relief. As soon as Pettigrew told him how the cargoes were rushed through to their final destination he calculated it would not take him long to discover what had become of the missing girl, for whom the big reward was offered.

Then, the fifty thousand for him, and perdition to the Eastern Queen.

At that moment the trampling of feet on the deck overhead told them that either some of the crew or the first part of the cargo had arrived. Pettigrew jerked his thumb upwards.

"Go up and see who it is," he said. "If it is the crew, kick them into the fo'castle, and keep them there; if it is the cargo, take charge and put them away. Here are the keys."

He tossed over a bunch of keys to his new second mate, and picking them up, Rymer made his way up the companion to the deck.

At the very top he met Sam Loo himself, and leaning heavily against his arm was the figure of a woman. A few steps behind stood the old woman whom Rymer had seen back in the den.

"Quick!" said the Chinaman, as soon as he recognised Rymer. "Get her out of sight before anyone comes! The old woman goes with her to look after her."

"All right; come on," answered Rymer.

Turning, he led the way along the deck until he reached the forward hatchway. The hatch itself worked on a hinge, and this Rymer threw back. A ladder led downwards into the darkness of the hold, but the faint starlight disclosed the fact that a floor had been set in a few feet down.

Rymer put his leg over the edge, and descended a few rungs, then clinging on with his right hand he held up his left arm for the captive. Sam Loo picked her up and lowered her until Rymer caught her, and steadied her over his shoulder. In this fashion he descended the rest of the way, and stood away from the bottom of the ladder until first the old woman, and then Sam Loo, had descended.

With his burden still over his shoulder, Rymer led the way along the rough flooring until he came to a door. Into the lock of this he fitted several keys until he found the right one. When the door swung open it revealed a small cabin at the opposite end of which could be seen a half-open door leading into another cabin.

Evidently these were to be the quarters of the intended wife of the Governor of Hamai and her duenna.

The new second mate of the Eastern Queen moved on into the inner cabin. Then he laid his burden down on a couch. As her head went back on the pillow her eyes opened for a moment.

Although they met Rymer's fairly, there was no recognition in them nor, in fact any cognisance of her surroundings, for the drug still held her in its grip.

It was more of a mechanical action of the lids as the change of posture was subconsciously felt. The fact that they had opened, however, had wrought a swift change in the appearance of her features.

Before, they had been coldly perfect, but without the finish of expression and touch of life which the open eye gives to the face.

Back in Sam Loo's place Rymer had gazed upon the still features with the others, but then they had stirred no chord of memory. Now, however, the eyes had lent a familiar touch to the face; but before he could be quite sure the lids had dropped, and it was again a cold mask.

He straightened up as Sam Loo's voice sounded. He was speaking in English to the old woman, who would accompany the captive.

"You look after her," he said curtly. "Keep beside her every minute until you reach China. Then hand over the letter to His Excellency the Governor of Hamai. He will reward you and give you money to return. If you fail in your duty you had better never been born."

"Oh! you rest easy, my child," croaked the old hag, with a shrill cackle. "Old Mother Peters knows her duty, that she does. The bonnie lass will be safe with me until she becomes the happy bride of his Excellency."

Rymer interrupted her garrulousness with a gesture.

"I think, in order that not too many of the crew know of her presence on board, I had better see after her needs personally," he said. "The old woman can occupy the outer cabin, and if any curious eyes are about they will only see her."

"A good idea!" nodded the Celestial. "I can see, Mr. Mate, that you are a big asset to Captain Jonas Pettigrew. With all due respect to that excellent man, he needed just such a hand as yours aboard the Eastern Queen."

"They need firmness, and they will get it from me," grunted Rymer, as he led the way out.

For the next hour he was busy getting the thirty-nine Celestials who composed the cargo settled in the narrow quarters which were to serve them during the journey. Kelly, the mate, had rounded up the crew, and from the lot had managed to find a number sufficiently sober to work the ship down the channel.

As soon as he got an opportunity, Rymer sought the cabin aft which was now to be his quarters, and locking himself in, sat down to think.

The vague familiarity of that face had stirred his thoughts so persistently that he knew it had suggested no trivial occurrence in the past. Consequently, he was determined to search his memory until he put his finger on the incident. In the game upon which he was engaged, no coincidence obtruding itself from the outside could be neglected.

It was a strange medley of pictures over which his mind went as it delved into the past. All countries, all peoples, moments of opulence and months of poverty, carnage, and the smoke of battle, dark retreats and brilliant mansions, jails and prisons, flight and hiding, hunger and thirst, and plenty.

And then away back in the time when crime was fresh, even to him, he raked up the incident he sought and fitted it to the lovely face which had started the search.

It was during his presence in the Republic of Ante Rita, in South America, when Mademoiselle Yvonne was startling the world by her daring coups. President Pearson, of that country, was to be her next victim when she had met Rymer and invited him to join forces with her. Then, because he had disobeyed her, she had dismissed him.

Again Fate had thrown them together, but only for a brief interval. That was at the time of the abduction of John Strang, the American multi-millionaire, by Wu Ling. Then, Rymer had had his hands full to preserve his own skin. Now Fate had again thrown them together, and as he realised the startling truth, he rose and began pacing up and down.

"Has she fallen a victim to the System?" he muttered, "or is her capture voluntary, and only part of some deep purpose she has in view? Mademoiselle Yvonne does not strike me as the type to fall a victim to any System, and yet she is helpless and alone.

"Rymer, my boy, it strikes me you are getting into deep water; but if you can't snatch something out of it, you deserve to be shot. In any event, I shall keep my eyes open and see what her game is—if she has any. If not, and she is a victim, who knows, I may find her very useful."

With that he turned and sought the deck.

Looey Sing carried the intended wife of the Chinese
mandarin to his lonely hut.

KENNEDY, the American Secret Service man, arrived at Baker Street on Christmas morning sharp, at the hour Blake had named.

The consulting-room presented a more orderly appearance, due to the fact that Mrs. Bardell had taken advantage of the early morning hours to bring some sort of order out of the confusion the litter of presents had caused. Blake was toasting his feet before a cheerful fire, a pipe in his mouth, and a book on his knees.

He rose at once as Kennedy entered, and while Tinker took the visitor's coat and hat, and passed them out to Mrs. Bardell, led the American over to a big easy chair beside his own.

"You are cosy here," smiled Kennedy, sitting down with an air of contentment and taking a cigar from the box Blake held out. "It's cold outside."

"I judge so, from the turned-up collars of the passers-by," said Blake, with an answering smile. "Anything new regarding the matter of which we were speaking yesterday afternoon?"

Kennedy shook his head.

"Not a blessed thing. I was in hopes that array of grey matter you possess would evolve some more brilliant, suggestion."

"I am afraid I have been doing a good deal of thinking regarding other things," laughed Blake. "My mind has been occupied with an incident which occurred soon after you left, yesterday. And, in a way, it is a bit of a coincidence."

"Indeed! In what way?"

"In that it brings in an element—though to be sure but remotely—which yours contains, or I should say, which composes the main structure of yours."

"What—Celestial?"

"Exactly. It is a curious story in a way, and oddly enough the first point of investigation regarding it begins at one of the places we spoke of—Cardiff."

"Then you have accepted it as a case?"

"Yes, principally because it presents an interesting professional phase, and furthermore, because the investigation of it will not conflict at present with your problem. Then, if as I hope, we clear up the matters which are bothering you, I shall continue until I succeed—

or fail. If you are interested, I will give you an outline of it, in so far as it has any bearing on matters Celestial."

"I should be very pleased to hear it."

Blake leaned back and began speaking in short, terse sentences. He sketched a rough description of the case up to the point where it brought in the journey of the Duke of Carrisbrooke and his family to Peking. Then he dwelt more in detail on the subject, and when he detailed the disappearance of the Lady Sybil, in Cardiff, it did not take much to see that Kennedy was highly interested.

"By ginger!" he exclaimed, when Blake had finished. "That is an interesting case, from a professional point of view. But what on earth possessed them to let two weeks go by before consulting you?"

"A misconceived notion that amateurish methods would locate her," answered Blake, with a shrug.

"It was a mistake—a big mistake. At the same time, I can tell you a little something about that game, it is this: the Chinese who are in California often take back wives on their return to China, and to my knowledge a good many of those wives have been imported for them from Europe.

"Now, as you say, the missing girl may have been taken direct to the East if this incident regarding Pekin is the explanation of her disappearance. On the other hand, your theory that she may have gone via America, strikes me as more probable. If she is gone that way, it is a safe bet that she has been taken by the same underground system by which the Chinese are finding their way into the States. In that case, the investigation will certainly run parallel for a certain distance.

"I have never been put on the investigation of matters Chinese in California, but I know this thing goes on, though by what route it is worked I haven't the faintest notion. In fact, as I told you when I came, the whole proposition is an absolute mystery to me."

"And it is a mystery which we must set ourselves to clear up without delay," said Blake quietly.

Then he turned to Tinker.

"Bring me the book of charts, my lad; also volume nine of the Index."

He drew a table between his chair and that of his visitor, and, when Tinker brought the articles he required, he laid the book on his knees and opened up the charts.

Kennedy bent forward, and for two solid hours those two giants of their profession pored over maps and notes from the Index, considering every possible route having advantages which might attract an underground system which wished to evade the eagle eye of the law.

Certainly, it must be a route presenting many things strongly in favour of evasion, for no inspection is more rigid in every way than that of the Customs and Immigration officials of the United States.

At the end of two hours Mrs. Bardell announced dinner, for Blake had changed the hour of that meal to midday, in order that Tinker might realise his anticipations regarding the "gobbler," before they left for Cardiff. Kennedy yielded to Blake's insistence that he should remain, and the three moved in with Pedro coming along behind, sniffing the air with a pleasant anticipation.

The feast was fully up to the expectations of both the lad and the bloodhound, and when it became absolutely impossible to continue a further attack on the good things, Tinker leaned back with a happy, and at the same time regretful, sigh.

After dinner Blake and Kennedy renewed their discussion, and at three sharp Blake stood up.

"I think it will be the best plan to motor through to Cardiff instead of going by rail. How do you feel about it, Mr. Kennedy?"

"I am in your hands while I am here," replied the latter. "By all means let us motor if you think best," Blake turned to Tinker.

"Ring up the garage, my lad, and order the car to be sent round."

"I think in that case I will get a taxi and go on to the hotel for my bag. I shall be back in twenty minutes," said Kennedy.

"All right," answered Blake. "In the meantime, I shall be getting a few things together myself."

True to his promise, Kennedy was back in twenty minutes exactly. While he had been gone, Blake and Tinker had packed their bags, the former taking the precaution to put in a disguise he had used during the past five months a great deal.

It was the disguise of a Chinaman, and those who have followed the records of Sexton Blake's journeys into the different Chinese districts of the big cities of the world, as well as into the heart of China itself, will know how perfectly he carried it off.

It was just half-past three when Blake dismissed the chauffeur and himself took the driving-wheel. Tinker and Kennedy were in the tonneau, with Pedro at their feet. Blake occupied the front seat alone.

Then, throwing in the clutch, the detective turned the car and headed for the country on their long drive, totally unaware that only a few hours before Yvonne had ridden over that same road, to put into operation her daring plan which was to have a far different ending from that which she herself had intended it should have.

They made better time on the journey than did Yvonne, for they had the last of the daylight during the first part of the journey and, though darkness, no rain on the latter part, as had the other car.

Consequently, they reached Cardiff a little after eight, having made not a single stop on the way. Like Yvonne, Blake drove to the Hotel North, for he had a desire to start his investigations regarding the disappearance of Lady Sybil from the place where she had been staying when it occurred.

When searching for the genesis of any crime, Blake almost invariably found inspiration for its reconstruction in the spot where it had its inception.

As the three of them descended from the car and started to enter, Tinker gave an exclamation of incredulity which caused Blake and Kennedy to swing sharply. There, coming along the street, was Graves—or, at least, the face was that of Graves.

His clothes were the clothes of a dock labourer, and looked oddly incongruous on the usually immaculate man who wore them. Tinker's exclamation caused him to glance up also, and a look of intense relief appeared in his eyes as he recognised Blake.

Hastening forward, he held out his hand.

"Thank heaven, you have arrived!" he said fervently. "I was just going to send you a wire."

Blake shook hands with him and presented him to Kennedy.

"It is a surprise to see you here," he said, knitting his brows. "I thought you and Mademoiselle Yvonne either at Queen Anne's Gate or on your way to the Mediterranean. But we can't talk here, and from your expression I judge something serious has happened. Come into the hotel."

"Yes, I can't tell you here," answered Graves. "I am staying at the North myself. Have you dined?"

"No, we are going direct to the dining-room."

"In that case I will join you there shortly. It will take me only a few minutes to change."

They moved on into the hotel, and while Graves hurried up to his room the others made their way to the desk in order to register, and then on into the dining-room.

Needless to say, Blake was deeply puzzled over the unexpected discovery of the presence of Graves in Cardiff. His first thought was that it had some bearing on what he had told to Yvonne, and that therein he would find an explanation of the strange occurrence.

In that he was right.

Exercised as was his mind over the matter, he became silent, and neither of the others interrupted his chain of thought. Kennedy was endeavouring to puzzle out who Graves was and what connection he might have with his own case; and as for Tinker, he knew the signs too well to interrupt.

Ten minutes after they sat down, a very different looking Graves appeared, though the expression of worry in his eyes had by no means departed. He gave his order jerkily, and turned to Blake.

"I am afraid something very serious has happened."

"I shall be glad to hear the details at once, if you don't mind," answered Blake quickly. "You can speak before Mr. Kennedy with perfect freedom."

"I'll begin at the moment when you and Tinker left Queen Anne's Gate on Christmas Eve," went on Graves, after taking a gulp of wine.

Without pausing, he went on to relate all that had happened from that moment until Yvonne, in the garb of a country girl, left the Hotel North earlier in the evening. He paused at that point to take another gulp of wine, then he resumed:

"Alec and I followed her as she wished. I hated the whole proposition, and was dead against it from the start; but she would do as she had planned, and you know how hopeless it is to oppose her when her mind is made up."

Blake nodded.

"I know. Go on."

"Well, she hadn't got very far into the district when a man approached her and, we judged, asked her if she had lost her way. We saw Yvonne nod her head, and after a few more words start off with him. We followed at a distance. They turned up a dark side street, and some way up, stopped before a house of some sort. At that moment we saw the man throw his arm about Yvonne's throat, and a moment later she collapsed. That meant drug, and as such a move wasn't in the programme, both Alec and I started forward to rescue her.

"As we did so, another man in seafaring costume hurried by, and before we reached the spot the whole three of them had disappeared into the house. We drew off, and debated what we should do. Alec was for entering and demanding her, for it looked to us as though she had got into a pretty tough joint, and the fact that she was drugged to get her there caused me to feel mighty nervous.

"She is clever, but in a condition of coma she is just as helpless as anyone else. I thought an entrance might do little good and only alarm them. That would mean the hastening of whatever fate was in store for her. Anyway, I decided to move cautiously, and then it occurred to me that I would send you a wire telling you in detail what had happened. I left Alec on the watch, and came round to do so. Well—I met you at the very door of the hotel. That is all."

Blake had listened tensely to every word Graves had uttered. When he finished the detective leaned back with a strange look in his eye.

"It was cleverly thought out," he muttered, more to himself than for the benefit of the others. "If anything would show what channel was used for the kidnapping of the Lady Sybil, that would do so. But, my heavens, what deadly danger she is in!

"It was foolish and reckless in the extreme. There is only one chance in a thousand of such a plan succeeding. The idea of having the yacht sent here was good, and it may prove a tremendous asset before we have finished with this affair. But Chinese, the Lady Sybil, everything, will have to be shelved for the moment. Yvonne must be saved. An entry by Graves and Alec would have precipitated matters at once. Force is useless in a case of this kind. Strategy must be employed if I am to succeed."

As he reached this point in his musings, Blake looked up.

"You do not know if the Fleur-de-Lys has yet arrived?" he asked curtly.

Graves shook his head.

"No, but I think not. Had it done so, Captain Vaughan would have come here at once to report. Yvonne said he would be here to-night, though."

"The wisest thing you ever did was to refrain from entering that place. As you say, it would have brought matters to a very unpleasant pass for Yvonne. The mistake you made, however, was in not communicating with me the moment she expressed her intention of doing such a thing."

"I didn't dare!" replied Graves. "By the way, you said in your note which accompanied that jade sphere that she should keep it in a safe place."

Blake leaned forward suddenly.

"Yes!" he snapped. "What about it?"

"Well, I am wondering if there is any chance of that being seen. She put it in a chamois bag and hung it for safety on the chain about her neck. It was concealed, though, by her bodice."

"My heavens!" gasped Blake hoarsely. "Yvonne in the hands of Celestials, and in possession of the Sacred Sphere of the Son of Heaven. It means either her death or, by a very long chance, her lifelong imprisonment, as something sacred herself, which would be worse than death. This is awful! I must do something without delay. If you have all finished we will go to my room."

As they had done so they rose and followed Blake, who was already half way towards the door. They almost had to break into a trot to catch him up, so swiftly did he walk, and, in fact, he had to hold the lift a moment until they came along. In his sitting-room Blake waved them to chairs, and kept on into his bed-room without any explanation.

Ten minutes later he came out again. When he did so Kennedy and Graves shot up from their chairs in amazement, and serious though the affair was, a furtive grin passed over Tinker's features.

Well he knew the disguise in which Blake was attired.

It was the disguise of a Chinese coolie, coarse and simple. His face was a perfect reproduction of the Celestial type, and his eyes looked as slant-set and as heavy-lidded as those of any Chinaman out of Canton. His shuffle was perfect; his bearing superb.

He approached Kennedy and spoke briefly.

"I am sorry it has become necessary to put into operation the plan I had intended, before we had spied out the land," he said. "However, you will understand the necessity. The young woman who has gone into the jaws of that den is a very old friend of mine and, I may say, dear to me. I should never forgive myself if I did not do all in my power to rescue her."

A strange quiver entered Blake's voice for a moment, but when he next spoke it was gone. Even when a thing touched himself, he realised that for all practical purposes he must be the cold analytical machine. To be anything else would cause his better judgment to be in danger of becoming blurred by the dictates of his heart, which told him to gather together a force and and the place without delay.

But Blake had too intimate an acquaintance with the Chinese and their ways not to know full well that there were probably half a dozen underground exits from the den by which the occupants would all escape were a raid made. They could easily enter, but the place would be empty, with probably a sleepy Celestial behind the bar and a seaman or two drinking beer. The wiles of the Celestial must be met and conquered by wiles. It remained to be seen if Sexton Blake could do it—in time!

"My plan is that I go on at once to the street where she disappeared," he said, after a moment's pause. "Graves will show me the way. I think you and Tinker had better remain here and be ready for any message; also you can be on the look-out for Captain Vaughan—Tinker knows him. I will leave Graves and Alec outside, and enter the place. I may be in there an hour, I may be until daylight, and, if my identity is discovered, I may never get out. However, do nothing until daylight. If I am all right, I shall have communicated with you before then."

"I shall, of course, follow your lead, Mr. Blake," said Kennedy, with a faint tinge of disappointment, though he was too experienced a detective himself not to realise the truth and force of the other's statements. "I should dearly love to take an active hand with you, but I daresay I shall be of more use outside. In any event, I can obey orders as well as give them. Tinker and I will remain here every moment until daylight. If you send word for any move to be made, you can depend on its being done to the best of our ability."

"You certainly can," exclaimed Tinker.

"Good!" said Blake. "With you and Tinker here, and Graves and Alec outside, I shall feel that I have something dependable behind me. By the way, Graves, you had better write a note to Captain Vaughan before we leave, instructing him to keep up full steam. It is impossible to tell where things are going to wind up, and in a case of this kind we need every aid we can lay our hands on. You, Tinker, send word to the garage to have the car made ready for immediate use. Have the lamps refilled, and petrol put in. We will neglect no precaution; then we shall have no regrets."

While he had been speaking, Graves had written a hasty note to Captain Vaughan, which he passed over to Tinker. A moment later he and Blake departed, leaving Kennedy and Tinker to carry out their part while he entered the den of the yellow tiger and pitted his wits against those of the wiliest race which has ever evolved from our ancient Simian ancestors.

Graves, spurred on by his anxiety regarding Yvonne, walked at a pace which satisfied even Blake. In less than a quarter of an hour he had turned up a dark street and indicated a house far along in the shadow.

"That is the place," he said, in a low tone.

Blake, who had been walking with head bowed, looked up.

"That," he said, in a soft tone which was almost icy with suggestion, "that is Sam Loo's place, and Sam Loo is one of the wiliest Celestials out of China. We indeed have our hands full to outpoint that gentleman. But one thing is proved. It is no common den into which Yvonne was taken. If anywhere we are apt to find traces of the secret underground system which we know exists, then at no more likely spot could we begin. It was at Sam Loo's I had intended making a start.

"On the other hand, if it is discovered that Yvonne is in possession of the Sacred Sphere, for which every Celestial has been on the watch for two hundred and fifty years, then no man can tell her fate. But here comes someone. Is it Alec?"

Graves peered ahead at a shadowy figure which was looming up from in front.

"Yes," he answered, after a moment. "It is Alec."

Blake draw up and laid a hand on the arm of the other.

"We will wait for him. It will be best not to be seen congregated outside Sam Loo's."

Owing to the fact that Blake was wearing a long, heavy coat, Alec did not see that he was apparently a Chinaman until he drew close; then he gazed in amazement. Graves cut short the question which sprang to his lips. "This is Mr. Blake," he said quickly. "Anything new?"

"Not a thing, Mr. Graves. After you left three men came out of the door through which Mademoiselle Yvonne disappeared. They looked like seamen from one of the ships, and after talking for a bit, one of them went one way, and the other two in a different direction.

One of that pair looked like the man who entered the place immediately after Mademoiselle Yvonne, but I wasn't positive."

"It makes no difference," put in Blake. "The main point is that she has not been brought out of the door by which she entered. That means she is either in there yet, or that she had been got away by another exit. Tell Alec what I have planned to do, Mr. Graves, and be sure you keep the watch every minute. If I have any message to send to Kennedy I will communicate with you in some way. You had better keep this coat for me. It is of a better quality than a lower class Chinaman would wear, and little things like that must be taken into account."

He was slipping off the coat while he was speaking, and, after tossing it across to Graves, drew out a cigarette and lighted it. That done, he nodded briefly to the other two, and passed up the street at a shuffle, heading for the public room of Sam Loo's joint.

This part of the place was as innocent in appearance and reality as the public bar of any other place in Cardiff. It was cut up into three sections to which any man, habitue or stranger, had entrance. There spirits, wines, and beers were served, and were of as good a quality as the law intended they should be. Like most saloons, it did a good trade, and, being in a choice location, had a particularly large clientele from the ships in port, a clientele which spent well and was easily pleased.

It served Sam Loo as a regular place of business, and had the greed of that cunning Celestial not driven him on to devise ways of breaking international law, he would have done well enough just the same, for the bar paid a handsome profit.

Beyond the last section of the main bar ranged several small rooms, much patronised by mates and captains, particularly of the ilk which handled Sam Loo's cargoes. Into these the stranger or the police rarely penetrated, though they would have seen nothing of a compromising nature had they done so. It was at the end of the passage off which these rooms opened that the true inner life of Sam Loo's joint existed.

Locked on the inner side, the passage door defied entrance by the uninitiated did they by any chance wander that far—which was unlikely. Night and day a Celestial sat on the other side of the door, ready to open to any who gave the password; but having an electric button near his hand which he would press did anything of an alarming nature occur.

From where he sat he could look into the gambling-room, which was crowded day and night by sea captains and sailors of every nationality, and from every part of the globe, Chinese from the district, negroes, Portuguese, Spaniards, Dutch, Swedes, Americans, English, Irish, and even Scotch. The gambling-room might have been called the first step towards the inner sanctum of the den, but an entry to it by no means meant the privilege of proceeding further.

Beyond this room ran another passage which led to the opium room, a room closely guarded by two Celestials. Into that room many men passed in to hit the pipe, and spend the hours in fevered dreams of crimson hues, but to wake to the full cold reality.

It, like the gambling-room, was unusually full. Beyond it, again, was another passage, and this led to the private quarters of Sam Loo, where that gentleman transacted the multitudinous details of his extensive interests, received those with whom he had business of a particularly private nature, concealed his human cargoes, even made away with human beings did the necessity arise, and, in fact, lived the secret existence of a man whose wealth is gained by the despoiling of his fellows, whose ways are the ways of night, whose power is felt but seldom seen.

And it was into the web presided over by this watchful spider that Blake went. Little attention was paid to him in the outer bar. Such patrons were common there.

He shuffled along to the bar where a group of other Celestials stood, and barely lifted his heavy-lidded eyes as he asked for a drink. He spoke in the pure dialect of Southern China, and as most of the Celestials made it a custom to speak in English, no matter how broken, his use of the native tongue brought the attention of his immediate neighbours to Blake, which was exactly what he wished.

He gave not the slightest sign that he noticed their looks, however, but when he paid for his drink he pulled out a handful of gold from which he took a sovereign. The eyes of the other Celestials dropped to hide the avaricious gleam which had entered them as they saw the gold, but still the newcomer stood impassively sipping at his drink.

After a few moments one of them turned and spoke in Chinese.

"You come from the south?" he asked.

Blake nodded his head slowly.

"Canton," he said briefly, and returned to his drink.

"You just arrived?" persisted the other.

Then Blake lifted his head, and his sleepy eyes examined his neighbour before replying. His attitude was a perfect reproduction of the new arrival who was determined to be cautious with strangers, even though they were of his own nationality.

"You from the south?" he asked in his turn, ignoring the second question.

The other nodded.

"Yes. Canton."

"You been here long?" went on Blake.

"No. Six months. I come over from London."

Blake returned to his drink.

"I, too," he said briefly. "You know Han Wau in Canton?"

The other turned quickly.

"Han Wau I know well. He is the husband of my unworthy sister."

"In that case, you must be a particularly choice rascal," reflected Blake, "for Han Wau is one of the biggest sharks in the city of Canton."

Aloud he said:

"I know Han Wau very well. Been in his place plenty of times."

"What you come here for?"

The newly-arrived Cantonese shrugged, and then looked around carefully.

"I come from London to see Sam Loo. You know Sam Loo well?"

"Like a brother."

"You take me to see him?"

"How much?"

"One—two gold pieces?"

"Three."

"All right. You take me. I give you three."

"When, you want to see him?"

"To-night."

"All right. You wait here. I go to see if he speak with you."

Blake returned to his drink, while his newfound acquaintance made his way through the many devious passages until he reached the door leading into Sam Loo's private quarters. In about ten minutes he was back.

Blake still stood as impassive as ever, his eyes gazing at the counter before him as though he were oblivious of all that went on around him. His new acquaintance now announced that Sam Loo would see him.

"What your name?" he added.

"My name is Chen Foo," answered Blake. "And yours?"

"They call me Wou," answered the other. "Now you give me three gold pieces, I take you to Sam Loo."

Blake dug his hand into the pocket of his loose coolie trousers, and drew out the requisite number of sovereigns.

Wou snatched at them greedily; then turned.

"You follow me," he ordered.

And together they started through the bar towards the passage leading past the private rooms.

At the door which admitted them to the opium room Wou paused.

"If Sam Loo ask you, you say you know me well in Canton. I tell him you old friend of mine and Han Wau."

"All right," answered Chen Foo. "You old friend of mine."

He kept as close as possible to Wou whilst the latter rapped lightly on the door at the end of the passage. He was anxious to know what password admitted one to the inner sanctum of the joint, and from Wou's confident bearing he felt satisfied the latter was one of the best-informed habitues of the place. It began to look as if his carefully-made plan might work to some extent at least.

In answer to the knock a sliding panel, which Blake would almost have sworn did not exist had he not seen it, opened, and a yellow face filled the space like a hideous sketch in a cramped frame.

Wou uttered the one word "Cardiff" and Blake knew he had the password. The panel closed without the slightest noise, the door swung open with a barely perceptible click, and they passed through.

Along the dim perspective of the passage Blake saw the entrance to the gambling-room, and towards this Wou led the way. It was crowded as usual. Several different games were in progress, including poker, faro, fan-tan, and roulette, though perhaps the faro table claimed the largest number.

The air was heavy with the smoke of many pipes, cigars, and cigarettes; the smell of spirits and beer hung persistently over all; several boys hurried to and fro bringing drinks. It was a typical gambling joint.

Without pausing Wou passed through to the pipe-room, with Blake at his heels. Passing along between the rows of devotees who lay in all stages of mental saturation from the drug, they entered the passage leading to Sam Loo's private quarters.

There Wou tapped lightly on the door. A guttural voice bade them enter, a soft click followed as the lock was released from the other side, and at last Blake stood before Sam Loo himself.

As he returned the look of the latter, he endeavoured to trace some indication in the face of the Celestial of the undoubted ability he possessed; but beyond a hint of capacity in the broad, high forehead, he saw nothing of a striking nature.

Sam Loo looked not unlike countless thousands of other Chinamen who had come to the Occident years before, made money and started for themselves, increasing their legitimate profits by dealing in illegal goods.

Most profitable of all is the transportation of their own countrymen into countries where their entry is prohibited; and not only into the United States do they manage to get, but it is beyond question that vast numbers of prohibited Chinese find their way into Australia, via the lonely and unguarded coast of the great northern territory.

The Celestial studied the man whom Wou had brought to see him; then he waved his hand.

"You go out, Wou!" he ordered. "I talk with your friend!"

Wou turned at once, and the door closed behind him. When the sound of his shuffling footsteps had died away, Sam Loo looked up again.

"What you want, Chen Foo?"

"I come to Cardiff because I hear I can get to America," answered Blake in Cantonese. "I hear the great Sam Loo get me through."

"Who tell you?"

"I hear about it," said Blake evasively. "Maybe Kan Wau in Canton tell me."

"Eh—eh? You know it will cost much money?"

"How much it cost me?"

"Much—much! You speak English?"

"I speak Chinese," answered Blake.

"You must learn English. All Chinese who live in America have to speak English. Otherwise they run great risk. What, you pay to go?"

"One hundred gold pieces," answered Blake, with a well-feigned air of caution.

"Not enough. It will cost you three hundred gold pieces."

"All right. I pay you three hundred gold pieces if you get me through. But I want to go at once."

"Impossible. If you had come in one day sooner I could have managed it. As it is, you must wait for one week, ten days, maybe two weeks."

"I pay more to go at once," said Blake, with Oriental calm, though inwardly his heart had quickened at Sam Loo's remark.

If he could have been sent one day sooner had he come in, it meant that Sam Loo must have disposed of a batch that very day—perhaps that very night. If he had, it was almost a certainty that Yvonne would have been included; for, safe though he might consider himself, Sam Loo would never make the mistake of keeping her in England longer than he could help.

Anyway, one thing was certain—Sam Loo was a participant in the great underground system; and though that was a very small discovery in comparison with the whole length of the channel used, still it was a beginning; and with even a small beginning, Sexton Blake felt he was on solid ground, and stood a fighting chance of ferreting out the rest of the affair.

His idea that the investigation of Kennedy's problem, and the search for the missing Lady Sybil would run parallel for a certain distance, had proved correct; and that being so, it pointed to a strong connection between the genesis of each.

Yvonne's daring plan had undoubtedly been a clever method of reproducing the disappearance of Lady Sybil—and, as it happened, had been Blake's own idea of what he should do.

It had struck him at the time that a woman would be a great asset, but he had never voiced his thought. It had presented too much danger to be considered for a moment. And now Yvonne's act had placed her in that very situation. Above all was her danger increased a thousandfold by her possession of the Sacred Sphere.

All things considered, it was not at all surprising that his endeavour to save Yvonne should form the index finger which pointed to the existing parallel of the other two cases. Altogether, it was a curious mixture of Chinese cunning and, if he were ever to reach the end of his quest, Blake knew he would need all his wits about him. But the question of Yvonne's safety was, to his mind, the most pressing matter of all.

If she had already left Sam Loo's place, and was now aboard some vessel which would take her out of England, and decrease the chances of helping her, then if he failed, it would mean her disappearance for ever. Of that he felt certain. And impelled, also, by the feeling that his search for her would lead him toward, rather than away from, the solution of the other two cases, he made up his mind to fight hard in order to induce Sam Loo to ship him that very night, cost what it might.

All this providing it was not already too late. In that case it would be a stern chase with the yacht as soon as he discovered the name of the ship; but if that course had to be followed, he swore he would, if necessary, scour every sea on the globe in his search.

Sam Loo had been sunk in thought for some time. Though Blake did not know it, he was wondering if the Eastern Queen had already sailed—and if not, could room be found for another man? This newcomer from Canton had money, and Sam Loo hated to let anything slip through his fingers. Besides, there was the extra freight he had paid on the girl to be made up.

"I tell you what I do," he said finally. "There is a batch going through to-night. Maybe they gone—maybe not. Anyway, I try to get you onboard; but it cost you five hundred gold pieces. If you pay that, I send for a taxi and me try. If me fail, I pay you back two hundred, and you wait for next ship."

For answer, the man known as Chen Foo thrust his hand inside his blue jacket and drew out a wad of notes, which made Sam Loo curse himself, for not having asked a higher figure. Chen Foo counted out five hundred pounds and passed them over, then returned the balance to his pocket.

"There is the money. Now you get me away."

Sam Loo carefully counted over the notes, and put them safely away. As soon as that was over, he rose quickly.

"You wait here. I go and make arrangements."

Blake nodded and sank into a chair, while the other opened a door and disappeared.

As soon as he was gone, Blake jerked a pencil and piece of paper from his pocket, and wrote as follows:

Graves.—I think Y. has already been taken away. I am being shipped through as one of them. I may fail. If so I will be at the hotel later. If not, you will know I have succeeded. I dare not risk asking the name of the boat, and as soon as I am aboard, shall no doubt be kept closely confined. If I don't return, find out the names of all vessels which have sailed for America to-night. The number should be very few indeed—if more than this one. Then have the yacht leave as soon as it arrives. Take Kennedy, Tinker, and Pedro, and follow; but don't make any move on the high seas, and keep out of sight on the horizon. She may be a steam vessel, and she may be sail. If the latter, the chase will be a slow one. Make for the port where she is bound, and call at the post-office there for news. I will arrange to have some word there instructing you what to do. Tell Kennedy that I am also on a strong scent regarding his matter. Kennedy is to take command of the party in my absence, as in a matter of this kind he knows from long experience what I want done, and how to do it. Be sure to make no blunders.—S. B."

Barely had he folded his note around a sovereign when Sam Loo hustled in, and announced that the taxi was waiting. Blake rose at once and followed him. If Graves and Alec had obeyed his orders, he should have no trouble in conveying his note to one of them as he went past.

Sam Loo led the way down a flight of stairs into a rough cellar. From there he went along a long underground passage, which terminated in another flight of steps. At the top the door opened into a plain room, and that in turn into a passage which led to a street-door. Blake could understand now why, if Yvonne had been taken away, her departure had not been seen by Graves and Alec.

The taxi was at the kerb, and they entered at once. Evidently the driver already had his instructions, for he drove off as soon as the door slammed. As they tore around the first corner and went past the front of Sam Loo's place, Blake leaned his elbow on the edge of the opened window in the door of the taxi, his hand hanging out in a careless manner. Though his eyes were half closed, he was searching the dark street carefully.

Suddenly a shadowy figure appeared on the kerb, less than two yards away from him. With a swift turn of the wrist Blake jerked the gold-weighted note from his hand, and as they sped by he heard the soft thud as it landed at the feet of the watcher.

Then they turned another corner, and the result lay in the lap of the gods.

●   ●   ●   ●   ●

It was the same moment in London.

In a luxuriously-furnished bed-room in a big City mansion, a white-bearded man turned restlessly in bed and opened his eyes. A woman, with white hair and proud features, sat in a low chair beside the table near by, on which stood a carefully shaded electric lamp. The sick man's trembling voice broke the silence as his eyes rested on the woman.

"Is there any news yet?" he asked, in a whisper.

The woman rose at once, and laid a cool hand on his forehead.

"Hush, dear!" she said soothingly, though her own voice trembled slightly, "No news yet; but Mr. Blake is on the case, and if anyone can find Sybil he can."

"Ah, Blake! I had forgotten. Yes, yes; if anyone can find her he can!"

And as the thought brought rest to his tortured mind, the Duke of Carrisbrooke little knew of the danger into which Blake was going at that moment, in his endeavour to save another girl as well as the Lady Sybil.

BLAKE SEES YVONNE.

Blake, disguised as a Chinese coolie, meets Yvonne during her morning exercise.

WHEN Rymer left his cabin after his astounding discovery that it was Mademoiselle Yvonne's face and no other which was recalled to him by the eyes of the helpless girl below, his mind was in such a whirl of puzzled amazement over the reason of her presence there that, for the moment, he was deaf, dumb, and blind to every external happening.

The crew of the Eastern Queen were already preparing to cast off. Men, scarcely yet sober from their Christmas debauch, were up aloft unreefing the frozen, icy sails; others struggled with the hawsers, which had frozen stiff during the cold days the Eastern Queen had been in dock.

If nothing else, Captain Jonas Pettigrew was a thorough sailor, and his hoarse voice rent the frosty night air like the reports of a pistol as he snapped out bawling orders to his men. The first mate was nowhere to be seen.

Rymer lent a hand mechanically, and as he kicked a slacking seaman, but five seconds after he had done so, he would not have remembered it, so absorbed was he in his own thoughts.

Consequently, it is not surprising that he paid little attention to a taxi which raced recklessly along the slippery quay, and drew up perilously near the edge. As he had not seen the mate since the latter had left him and the captain in the city, he put it down to the tardy arrival of that individual, with perhaps the tail-end of the crew.

He proceeded with his task of directing the work forward, and paid no more heed to the matter, until he saw Captain Jonas Pettigrew and Sam Loo approaching him along the deck. For one awful moment he wondered if the wily Celestial had in some way spotted his game, had put the captain wise, and that now the reckoning was come. His hand drifted close to his hip, but his face showed no signs of what he was thinking.

Pettigrew spoke while yet several feet away.

"I have sent the mate below to stow away the cargo," he said. "There are thirty-nine of them. They came along while you were looking after the other affair. Now, they are too crowded down there as it is, and three of them have been put in a place where there isn't room to swing a cat. We want room for one more. Sam Loo is very keen on getting him away. Can you fix up some place for him? Sam says he has money on him, and we might screw something out of him to let him come as a sort of favour."

Rymer knit his brows.

"The girl and the old woman occupy the only places," he said slowly. "There is a place near them containing spare sails. It could be dug out and would do, only one could overhear what was being said in the other place; and as the girl, when she becomes conscious, will speak to the old woman in English, it would be unwise. The less any outsiders know the better."

Sam Loo pushed forward.

"Then that is all right, Mr. Mate?" he said quickly. "The man I want to send doesn't speak a word of English. He's fresh from Canton and wants to get through to the States as quick as he can."

"In that case, I guess I can fix him up," rejoined Rymer. "You had better see him, captain, and tell him through Sam Loo that we will arrange, as a favour, for him to come if he coughs up fifty quid."

Pettigrew nodded.

"I'll attend to that. Will you have the place fixed up at once?"

It will be ready in ten minutes," answered Rymer. "I will do it myself."

He turned as he spoke, and made his way along to the forward hatch. Descending by the ladder, he went along past the place where he had put Yvonne, and kicked open a door, which opened into a rough sort of cabin, filled with a heterogeneous collection of sails, twine, and tools.

These Rymer dragged unceremoniously out, and, lighting a stump of candle left by the ship's carpenter, proceeded to fix up a rough sort of habitation for the last member of the human cargo.

A few old sails folded up and jumped on formed a makeshift bed, and, with the exception of putting in a bucket of water for drinking purposes, this was the extent of Rymer's preparation to receive the passenger.

Barely had he finished when footsteps sounded outside, and Captain Jonas Pettigrew appeared, leading a tall Celestial of impassive mien clad in coolie costume.

He stood silent by the door whilst Rymer kicked the last of his bedding into shape. Then he walked forward and surveyed his surroundings.

Whilst he was so occupied Rymer turned to the captain.

"Did you get his money?"

"Yes. He paid up like a lamb. He gave ten pounds extra, and got Sam Loo to make arrangements that he should have the same food we have aft. He is a particular cuss."

"I guess the richness of the food won't hurt him," retorted Rymer sarcastically. Then, to the new arrival, he said:

"Well, these are your quarters, Chink. If you don't like them don't kick, for in the first place it wouldn't do you any good, and, in the second place, it is all we have. You don't speak English, so you don't understand what I have said, but I guess you can grab what I mean."

The Chinaman never blinked an eye during Rymer's remarks, and, as far as one could tell, understood not a single word.

When Rymer had finished the Celestial uttered a few words in rapid Chinese, which neither Rymer nor the captain understood, though they both knew a little of the language.

A moment later they departed, leaving the Celestial alone.

He stood impassive as ever until the sound of their footsteps had died away; then he stepped softly to the door and turned the key. That done, he drew out a cigarette and lighted it, after which he sank down on the pile of sails which was to be his bed.

"So," he murmured softly, as the blue smoke curled upwards, "your passenger speaks no English, eh? Well, you have bled me freely between you; but if you don't repay me a thousand times over in more than money, then my name is not Sexton Blake.

"Undoubtedly, I have come aboard the ship which holds the balance of the human cargo, but the question is am I aboard the ship which holds Yvonne? That is the question which must be settled, and until I find the answer I shall not know whether my deductions have proved trustworthy, or whether I have come on a wild goose chase which will be the biggest farce on record. But I can't believe the different analyses which I have made are all wrong.

"It stands to reason that Sam Loo would rush Yvonne out of the country at the very first opportunity which offered, and even if she only fell into his hands this evening, why should that alter his procedure! He would certainly gain nothing by holding her there, and, by his own words, another ship is not leaving for at least a week.

"On the contrary, it seems to me that he would work doubly

quickly, for she was a totally unexpected addition to his cargo, and, seizing her as he did, he will think a hue-and-cry will be raised by morning. The more I think of it the more certain I feel that she was shipped away.

"But—and there is the crux of the whole matter—is she on this vessel or on another? If Sam Loo had a very large consignment of men to send away, it is just possible that two vessels may be leaving. However, that is one of the unknown cards in the game which must be risked if I am to play a lead. It is, at least, a relief to find I am not herded with the others. Truly money does a lot, even with the underground system, the pulse of which I think I am beginning to feel.

"Now for the second, and, probably, most surprising element which has entered into this strange affair, and may yet cause serious complications. If that man who passes a mate of the Eastern Queen, and who has arranged these luxurious quarters for me, isn't someone I have met before I shall begin to have no confidence in my memory. If I could have seen him without his hat I should have known in a moment. His beard hides the true mould of his features, and the brim of his hat shades his eyes. But those hands, that voice—whose are they?"

For the space of ten minutes Blake—or Chen Foo, as he was known—sat smoking, delving into the past in much the same way as Rymer had delved, when he endeavoured to recall the suggestion conveyed to him by Yvonne's features.

Slowly Blake was searching the mental gallery of faces which he possessed, and, in truth, it was no small one. One by one he fitted them to the frame of the mate, and added the hands and the voice; but one by one he rejected them, until suddenly one face loomed out of the mists of the past, and remained focussed by his mind.

That face he saw with the beard stripped from it. The hat was removed, and the high, intelligent forehead rose white above keen grey eyes, below which a straight, powerful nose was placed. The hands were white, not cut and bruised, as were those of the mate; but it was the hands beneath the marks of toil which Blake saw.

Lastly he fitted the voice to the picture he had woven from memory, the human voice, which is the greatest betrayer of him who would hide his identity.

And as the completed picture unfolded itself before him he saw that it was indeed the picture of one whom he knew well, one whom he had hounded and caught, one against whom he had been pitted, before—yea, and one to whom he had been lenient on more than one occasion.

It was the face of Dr. Huxton Rymer!

As he realised the startling truth Blake rose, and, pulling off his Chinese slippers, began pacing up and down his narrow quarters with the stealthy tread of a panther, thinking, thinking, thinking.

The creaking of blocks overhead and the heavy trampling of feet told him they were at last getting under way. The distant sound of lapping water reached his ears as the Eastern Queen slipped away from her moorings.

There was no port-hole in his quarters, but he knew it must be nearly dawn.

He had been pacing up and down for several hours, and the fresh candle which Rymer had put in the neck of a bottle was only half burned down. Glancing at his watch, he saw that it was just past six.

It seemed unbelievable that his thoughts had consumed so much time. But there it was. He had not had time to feel weary, so engrossed was he in attempting to read some meaning in the maze of bewildering facts which appeared before him.

Less than forty-eight hours had passed since the Duchess of Carrisbrooke had come to his apartments in Baker Street to ask his assistance. Since then developments had taken place with almost bewildering rapidity.

Yvonne's aid had been sought and promised. Then she had exceeded the limits which Blake had mentally placed upon her participation in the affair, and now she was heaven only knew where.

Captain Vaughan, on board the Fleur-de-Lys, was steaming with all speed around from Plymouth to Cardiff—perhaps had already arrived at the latter port.

Kennedy, Graves, Tinker, and Pedro were in Cardiff. Blake himself, disguised as a Chinaman, on his way, by an unknown route, to an unknown destination.

And, last of all, Dr. Huxton Rymer had suddenly been thrust into the complicated problem.

Where it might all end, what might be the finish to it, Blake did not attempt to fathom at this stage of the game. Of one thing only was he certain, and that was the strong indication that he had indeed inserted the thin end of the wedge of solution into the mysterious and complicated workings of the great underground system which trafficked in human beings and human souls.

That being so, it meant that as long as life lasted he would apply every faculty he possessed, as well as every material resource, to the clearing up of the affair, no matter what it cost in time, money, or mental strain, nor where it might eventually lead him, even though it might be into the jaws of the yellow tiger himself.

At that moment a sound caught his ear which caused him to bring up with a jerk and stand scarcely breathing. It seemed to come from the direction of the partition to his right, and, as a repetition of the sound proved this to be the case, he moved softly across and stood with his ear pressed close to the wall.

He could hear much more distinctly now, and it was evident that the sound, whatever it might be, came from the other side of the very partition against which he stood.

It was the sound of a human voice—nothing remarkable in itself, to be sure—but on board a vessel like the Eastern Queen it was remarkable, for it was the silvery voice of a woman, and the language in which she spoke was English.

Blake held his breath, so intent was he on hearing.

At last the faint, high-toned murmur rose to a louder pitch, and as its fine cadences passed through the partition to the listening man, a strange dry glitter came into the heavy-lidded eyes, the only visible indication of the exultant tempest which was raging beneath the calm exterior.

Only one woman in the world had that delicious hesitancy of speech, and that woman was Mademoiselle Yvonne.

Although the voice came from the other side of the partition, it was not close enough for Blake to distinguish the exact words.

He judged—and rightly—that it emanated from an inner cabin, the door of which must be partly open. It was probable that Yvonne was talking with someone rather than speaking to herself, and as the sound of a faint, cracked treble reached him Blake knew this was the case.

He passed his hand across his forehead, and gaped stupidly when he found it came away wet. Only then did he realise how tense had been the strain of hope, and how utterly repressed had been his every feeling.

At that very moment a knock came at the door, and, stepping across, he turned the key. He imagined it was someone with food, and his thought proved correct.

He had hardly expected to see Rymer again for some days, at least, thinking the cook's boy would be sent with his food. But, to his surprise, it was Rymer, and no other.

He entered abruptly, and set a dish of food on the floor. Then he departed without a word.

Blake stood motionless until the door closed behind him. As it did so he heard Rymer walk along and knock at the door next to Blake's.

With a spring the detective was across the cabin, and had turned the key in the door.

A second time he heard voices, and just reached the partition in time to hear Rymer say in English:

"Good-morning, Mother Peters! How is your charge this morning?"

Then came the old woman's voice in reply.

"The bonnie lass is well, sir—very well—and hungry, too. She has been asking this last half-hour for her breakfast. Ah, me! She'll make a bonnie bride when—"

"All right! All right!" snapped the second mate testily. "Breakfast is being prepared now. When it comes, and you have finished, bring your charge on deck. I have arranged that you both exercise in the mornings. The others will exercise during the afternoons. I myself will come to fetch you."

With that he slammed the door, and a wave of disappointment passed over Blake, for he was racking his brains for some means of communicating with Yvonne. As long as the old woman was with her that would be well-nigh impossible. However, all he could do was to watch his chance and seize it if it came.

He judged from what he had heard Rymer say that he, in common with other Celestials, would only exercise during the afternoon. If Yvonne went on deck in the morning, that meant he would not even catch a glimpse of her; but he drew consolation from the thought that his deduction had led him to her unerringly, and time might provide an opening.

Judge of his surprise, therefore, when, after he had finished the plate of food Rymer appeared and jerked his hand towards the deck.

"You are to go up for exercise," he said, "and if you don't understand what I mean, you had better hurry up and do so."

Blake made a few gesticulations which were intended to convey the fact that he understood those of the other, and a moment later he was following in Rymer's wake, on his way to the deck. Evidently his extra payment had achieved him a certain amount of favour over the other Celestials.

On reaching the deck he walked at once to the side, and stood gazing across the stretch of water at the distant coast of Devon. A fair wind was carrying them down the Bristol Channel at a spanking pace, and Captain Jonas Pettigrew had taken advantage of it by clapping on every inch of sail.

Off to starboard could be seen the coast of South Wales, just emerging from the morning mist. All about them were several trawlers out of Bideford, Ilfracombe and Clovelly, little dreaming of the cargo the scudding Eastern Queen bore as she went past.

Straight ahead loomed the desolate Isle of Lundy, whose two brilliant lights had now gone out until another night should come.

Further on was Hartland Point, stretching away from Gallantry Bower until it broke suddenly and swung south-west to merge in the rocky and dangerous coast to Land's End.

Behind them, on the port side, lay Bideford Bar, guarding the entrance to the Taw and Torridge, and further still, Morte Point, where many a ship has gone to destruction in the teeth of the northern gales which sweep the coast. Swansea was a faint cloud to starboard.

A great thoroughfare is the Bristol Channel, and a great watery thoroughfare has it been ever since man first navigated his rude dug-outs along the endless coast which bounds the British Isles.

There the Romans sailed their war galleys and built massive piers to receive the trade which they built up; there the Vikings and the Saxons fought and lost and conquered, to be conquered in turn by the implacable forces of Nature; there the richly laden galleons from Virginia and the West Indies sailed to Bideford with cargoes of tobacco and gold and silver; there Drake and Grenville sailed in the glorious days of the Good Queen Bess and the Spanish Main; and there the same indomitable Drake harried the fleeing ships of Philip's Armada until they sank or ran but to sink further on.

There the great ships of every age have sailed, bringing their cargoes from every port in the world, and always from the dim, vague past has the sea taken its toll—an insatiable monster who demands and gets what he demands.

Until now, Blake had made no attempt to discover if Yvonne were on deck. He felt that caution was the keynote while he was on board the Eastern Queen, for full well did he realise the sharp eyes which would unceasingly watch every move of his, be he cargo or not; for in the business of trafficking in human beings one has to be careful.

Footsteps approaching along the deck caused him to straighten up and turn. As his eyes wandered over the deck in Oriental impassivity he saw, not ten feet away, the figures of two women.

One was short and old and wizened, the other was taller and slim. Her face was concealed by a heavy veil, and her hair was almost hidden by a soft, crush hat; but in one place a tiny wisp of bronze gold escaped to the morning air, and Blake knew that his ears had not betrayed him.

It was indeed Yvonne.

Not by the slightest flicker of an eyelash did he betray the emotion which surged over him at the actual sight of the daring, reckless, lovable girl. Though he could not see her eyes on account of the veil, it seemed to him that they rested on him in passing, for her head was turned in his direction.

In any event, even if they had, she would never have recognised in the coarsely clad Chinaman standing by the side, the clean cut figure of the vigorous detective whom she little thought so near her.

Shortly, after they passed him Blake saw Rymer approach and stop them. The detective shifted his position, and brought his ear into a line with the trio along the deck.

In the noise of the rushing water along the sides and the creak of spars and cordage overhead, it was difficult to catch what Rymer said. Had it not been for the carrying properties of the latter's bell-like tones and the acoustic properties given by a ball-ring sail, it would have been impossible.

He addressed the old woman curtly.

"You can stay on deck a while longer, Mother Peters," he said looking straight into the hag's eyes. "Your charge has been on deck long enough. I will take her below."

"But I will go, too," answered the old woman. "Sam Loo he say not to leave her a minute."

"You are under my orders now, not Sam Loo's," snapped Rymer. "You do as I say."

As he spoke he moved, until he stood close to her, and Blake could have sworn he saw the dull gleam of a piece of gold as it passed from Rymer's hand to hers.

When she spoke again her voice was fawning and cringing, as are the voices of her kind.

"If you say I must, then I must," she said. "Only not long, sir, not too long. The bonnie lassie would be lonely without me."

She finished with a harsh cackle which made Blake's blood run cold. As yet the veiled girl had stood motionless and apparently unheeding the talk which was going on between the two. Blake could not tell whether Rymer's voice had awakened any old memory or not; but of this he was now sure, that Rymer had in some way spotted Yvonne's identity. That being so, it meant an increase to the already sufficient peril which surrounded her.

She made not the slightest objection as Rymer took her arm and led her towards a narrow companionway which was set about 'midships. It was obvious from this that the quarters where Blake and Yvonne had been placed contained two modes of ingress and egress, a fact worth noting for the future.

Barely had they disappeared from view when the sleepy-looking Celestial, who still leaned against the side turned and shuffled along forward. Reaching the forward hatch he stood and gazed for a moment over the bow.

Only a few of the crew were visible about the deck, and they were occupied in coiling ropes and slushing out the scuppers; the big Martinique negro sat in his galley on an upturned bucket, peeling potatoes, a man lounged over the wheel at the stern, and the first mate leaned over the rail of the poop deck.

Captain Jonas Pettigrew was evidently below, and Rymer had gone down the companion with Yvonne. The old woman still paced up and down the deck waiting for the permission of the second mate to return to her charge.

All this Blake saw as he slowly turned his heavy-lidded eyes, interested in nothing, as always; then he tossed away his cigarette and swung himself over the edge of the hatch. At any hazard, he intended being on hand when Rymer should interview Yvonne, and all signs pointed to the suggestion that such an interview was about to take place.

On his arrival at the foot of the ladder, Blake stood for a moment peering along in the direction of his quarters. The faint murmur of a deep voice reached him, and he knew Rymer had already reached Yvonne's quarters. There was no hint of the slushing shuffle in his walk as he moved noiselessly along.

Reaching the door leading into Yvonne's quarters he caught Rymer's voice more distinctly; a moment later he was past the danger zone and in the security of his own cabin. Swiftly he turned the key, and more swiftly still he hastened across to the partition.

There was a lull in the sound of Rymer's voice, but as Blake pressed his ear hard against the thin wood he heard Yvonne's voice, strangely weak.

"What is it you wish to say to me? Is it not enough that I am in your power, going I know not where? Why do you persecute me in this manner?"

A short pause followed, then Rymer's deep tones again sounded;

"There is no persecution intended, my dear young lady," he said suavely, "if you listen to reason. But since you ask me what I wish to say to you, Mademoiselle Yvonne Cartier, I will tell you."

Blake heard a startled exclamation as Yvonne's name dropped mockingly from Rymer's lips. Dead silence reigned for fully a minute. At the end of that time Yvonne's voice came calm and unruffled as of old.

"You seem to have the advantage of me, Mr. Mate. Perhaps you will be good enough to tell me who you are?"

"Then you do not deny that you are Mademoiselle Yvonne?"

"I admit nothing—I deny nothing."

"I am surprised that you haven't recognised me before this," went on Rymer. "We are really quite old friends, mademoiselle!"

"Indeed! I am afraid—oh! my memory serves me better now, Dr. Huxton Rymer. I had failed to notice your hands before. Now that we know on what footing we stand, perhaps you will explain your reason for coming here? From past experience I judge it is a proposition to sell some of your friends."

Blake's grim features broke into a fleeting smile as he heard Yvonne's sarcasm. It was very evident that that resourceful young lady was fast getting a grip on herself. Rymer's momentary silence proved the shot had told.

"It just happens that I am here to do nothing of the sort," he said at last. "What I am here for is to find out why you are aboard this ship bound for China to become the wife of a Celestial?"

"So I am bound for China, am I?" rejoined Yvonne. "Really, you are most obliging, Dr. Rymer. And I am to become the wife of a Celestial, am I? How delightful!"

"I guess any information I give you won't do any harm," said Rymer grimly. "You can joke about it if it gives you any consolation, but believe me, mademoiselle, you were never in a tighter place than you are right now. Whether you got here through some scheme of your own, or whether you were caught as others have been caught, I don't know, but I propose finding out before this voyage is over. In any event, you can take it from me that all your ingenuity will not get you clear without my assistance. That is straight. Moreover, I am prepared to give you that assistance providing you agree to my terms."

"Indeed! Might I inquire why you are so walling to help me, Dr. Rymer? If I remember rightly, you have no reason to be so."

"I will tell you."

Blake leaned close as he caught the tense tone of Rymer's words.

"Listen, Mademoiselle Yvonne! Away back in South America, when with my assistance you landed Jim Pearson for two millions, I would have been a loyal partner of yours. You thought otherwise, and we parted."

"When you disobeyed my orders by trying to murder Sexton Blake's assistant," broke in Yvonne.

"I tried to make him walk the plank, and would have made his master, too, if I had had the chance, for I hated them."

"Perhaps, but that gave you no excuse for disobeying."

"The reason for my hatred did. That reason was because I loved you, mademoiselle. I loved you from the first moment I met you at the President's ball in Santa Rita. I loved you while I worked with you. I have loved you since, and I love you now. For you I would do anything, if it would bring me your love in return. I would even run straight. That is the reason why I would help you now."

"If a man's love be worth having it is not the love which promises to perform on conditions. It is the love which gives all, asking nothing in return. That is a love which you never had nor ever could have, Dr. Rymer. Even if I needed your help I could not accept it for such a reason, for—I do not love you!"

"By heavens, let me tell you that whether you love me or not you will be my wife!" blazed Rymer. "I had a chance until Sexton Blake came on the scene. Why you should care for a man who had hounded you all over the globe, and even put you in prison, I can't see."

Then his voice changed to a curious note of pleading, and Blake felt almost guilty as he listened.

"Say you will marry me, Yvonne. I swear to you I will do everything you say. One word, and you make of me what you wish. You may theorise all you please about love, but I tell you I love you with every atom of my nature, and it is not a love to be baulked."

"And I have told you I do not love you, and never could love you," answered Yvonne. "If you meant half you say you would leave me alone. When I want your help I will ask for it."

"Then listen to me," said Rymer, in tones now deadly cold. "If you have come here on some scheme of your own you may think you have left traces which your confederates can follow. Let me undeceive you. When you were seized and taken into that joint in Cardiff I was immediately behind you. When you were taken out you were taken by a long underground passage which led into another street. Then you were put into a taxi and hurried down to this ship, which sailed the same night. So your friends could not trace you even were they as clever as Sexton Blake himself.

"When I tell you that, for once in your life you are helpless, and at the mercy of a system which never lets go its grip once they get a hold, I am not telling nonsense. Without my help you will go through to China as sure as the sun rises, and once there even I cannot help you. If you prefer to be the wife of a Celestial rather than be mine, that is a matter for your own taste. Only—and mark my words—either you marry me or you go to your fate."

"Even with all your boasted love you are not making me this offer without some private axe to grind," said Yvonne. "You must need my help in some plan of your own, and feel that it is a tremendous asset to you."

"I will be frank with you. I do need your help. I joined this ship for just one purpose. It is to locate a girl who has disappeared, for the reward is worth working for. With you helping me we could pull it off without a chance of failure, for now that you are started on the underground channel you are bound to go the same way she did. You could keep on until we were positive, then I would get you clear of it before you were taken out of 'Frisco."

"Your great love certainly doesn't prevent your permitting me to continue in the awful peril you have painted," remarked Yvonne cuttingly. "I am afraid I must refuse to entertain any such suggestion, Dr. Rymer. If I have got into this position of my own accord, rest assured I shall get out of it with the same success. On the other hand, if I am here as an unwilling captive, I think I shall be able to get free just the same. But be quite sure, Dr. Rymer, before anything forced me to become the wife, either of you or any Celestial, I should prefer to, and would, wed death.

"Now go, please. I am tired."

"All right," exclaimed Rymer furiously. "Have it your own way. We shall see if you get free."

The loud slamming of the door indicated that Rymer had gone off in high dudgeon, but still Blake stood with his ear against the partition.

Suddenly the sound of choking sobs broke out in the next cabin, followed by the jerky cadence of Yvonne's voice.

"He is right—he is right," she said, over and over again. "If they took me away from the place in Cardiff by another street, uncle would never know, and will think I am still there."

Her voice died away then, and Blake, with a silent step, drew away from the partition. Thrusting his hand in his pocket he drew out a lead pencil and again approached the wall. A moment later a soft, regular tapping sounded as he struck the end of the pencil lightly against the wood.

Had a Morse operator heard it he would have recognised it at once as the famous telegraphic code, and, moreover, he would have known that Blake was tapping over and over again the letters:

Y-v-o-n-n-e—Y-v-o-n-n-e—Y-v-o-n-n-e. Without stopping for a moment he kept this up, with his ear pressed against the wall. Fully ten times had he tapped out the word before the sound of sobs in the next cabin ceased, and a dead silence followed. Once more Blake struck the letters:

Y-v-o-n-n-e.

A moment later a faint noise reached him from the other side. Bending his head he deciphered the message which was being tapped:

I-n—h-e-a-v-e-n-s—n-a-m-e—w-h-o—a-r-e—y-o-u?

As the sentence finished Blake again raised the pencil and tapped out:

B-l-a-k-e.

Even through the partition he heard Yvonne's incredulous gasp; then the sound of her door came to him, and the sharp tones of the old woman broke out demanding to know what Yvonne was doing on the floor.

He did not wait to hear her answer, but thrust his pencil away and drew out a cigarette. He had achieved one important thing, anyway, and that was the conveying of the knowledge to Yvonne of his presence on board. That in itself was a good deal, and, if nothing more, would be a tremendous comfort to her.

Knowing her well though he did, Blake would never know of the great stab of exquisite pain which had shot through Yvonne as she heard the almost unbelievable fact of Blake's presence tapped out to her.

Stepping quietly to the pile of sails, Blake closed his eyes in thought. He made an odd picture as he sat there on the rough pile of sails, the flickering light of the candle falling on his yellow face, and his heavy-lidded eyes drooped over an impassive Celestial countenance.

But even when alone he did not permit himself to forget his role. One never knew where a hidden spyhole might exist, and he knew what his life would be worth did the faintest hint get to Rymer of the man who really existed beneath that yellow exterior.

Now that the game had moved another step he had much pondering to do, not least of which was a deep consideration of Rymer's startling proposal to Yvonne and his feverish declaration of love for her.

It was odd what a peculiar feeling made itself evident in the region of Blake's heart as this thought occurred. He had experienced it before when Rymer had been speaking, but had anyone suggested it might emanate from his own unacknowledged regard for that young lady he would have regarded them with pitying contempt.

It is a well-known fact that the cleverest lawyer looks after his own affairs very imperfectly. Was it possible that the brilliant detective who was so keen in his analyses of others, and the motives which governed them, could not analyse himself?

Be that as it may, it was certainly a fact that Yvonne's danger had spurred him on as no professional case had ever done.

•　　　•　　　•　　　•　　　•

Back in Cardiff things had been moving swiftly. It was Alec at whose feet Blake's gold-weighted message had fallen as the latter sped past in the taxi with Sam Loo. Yvonne's faithful fellow had picked it up, not comprehending at first that it might be Blake's promised message. Graves, who was on guard some distance up the street, saw Alec approaching and went to meet him.

"What is it?" he asked quickly.

"I dunno, Mr. Graves," answered Alec. "I was standing down there when that taxi went past. As it did so this was thrown from it and landed at my feet."

Graves eagerly took the note and handed the sovereign to Alec. They moved across to the rays of a sickly light which shone from a ship-chandler's shop near by, and there Graves spread out the note. As he took in the meaning of Blake's hurried message he turned sharply.

"It is from Blake," he said, with an unaccustomed vigour in his usually drawling tones. "He is on the trail. My heavens, what a man he is—what a genius! We must lose no time in getting back to the hotel."

They hurried off down the street, and, hailing a crawling four-wheeler, ordered the man to drive at once to the Hotel North. There they found Kennedy and Tinker waiting as had been arranged.

Graves passed the note at once to Kennedy, who read it, and in turn gave it to Tinker. When the lad had finished he looked up.

"Well, the guv'nor says he may not land what he is after," he said, "but I guess we might as well go ahead with what he suggests. If I am any judge he will land there with both feet."

Kennedy smiled at the lad's loyalty.

"I wish I could inspire such loyalty in my assistants," he said. "But you may be right. In any event we will be prepared. He says not to make any open move on any account, but to make it a stern chase. We will follow his instructions. He also suggests that I take command of matters in his absence. Are you all agreed?"

"I am," answered Tinker, "Anything the guv'nor says is good enough for me."

"I shall be very glad to have you do so," remarked Graves. "I can also answer for Alec."

"Then that is settled," said Kennedy. "Now to apportion out our work. Tinker will go to the docks and knock about picking up any gossip he can, regarding outgoing vessels. I will get into touch with one or two shipping men. It will be necessary to knock them up at their private houses, but I wish to get hold of a list of any vessels which are due to leave. I will endeavour to find a pilot. You, Mr. Graves, will remain here and await Captain Vaughan's arrival; then you can give him the necessary instructions. Perhaps it would be as well if Alec accompanied Tinker."

They all rose at once and began to prepare to carry out their different duties. Tinker departed with Alec, Kennedy sought his room for an overcoat, and Graves made his way to the lounge in order to meet Captain Vaughan when he came in.

The captain did not make his appearance until almost three in the morning, and looked extremely astonished to see Graves sitting waiting for him. Hard on his heels Kennedy came in, and the three talked over what was to be done. It seemed that Captain Vaughan had made port several hours before, but had not arrived at the hotel sooner owing to the fact that he had been attending to an injured sailor.

It was not until a little past six that Tinker and Alec returned. Kennedy glanced up eagerly as the lad approached.

"Well, Tinker, any news?"

"Very little, Mr. Kennedy," replied the lad, "but I am not so sure that it isn't what we want. No vessel left the harbour between six last night and six this morning. The Grace K. Williams, tramp steamer, bound from Cardiff for Rio, and loaded with coal, cleared at six last night. The next vessel to clear was the Eastern Queen, brigantine, loaded with coal and bound for St. John, New Brunswick. Those are the only two."

"Good boy!" cried Kennedy. "I found out about the Grace K. Williams myself, but the hour at which she cleared puts her out of reckoning. In my opinion, gentlemen, the Eastern Queen is our quarry. If you are all agreeable we will move in and have breakfast, then for the Fleur-de-Lys and a slow chase across the Atlantic."

THE SIXTH CHAPTER   BLAKE REGAINS THE SACRED SPHERE— AND IS TRANSSHIPPED.

IF Blake thought he would have many opportunities of communicating with Yvonne he was disappointed. Whether the old woman had become suspicious in any way at finding Yvonne on the floor he could not tell.

This much he did know, however. The hag left Yvonne alone not the smallest fraction of a second. Had Blake been less experienced he might have tried to bribe her, as he had seen Rymer do, but his knowledge of the type told him that did he try such a proceeding it would be a colossal mistake.

She had taken Rymer's gold, it is true, but it had been only because she knew he would have his way in any event. The only individual to whom she would be loyal was the man who gave her her living—Sam Loo—and that not out of love, but from a wholesome desire to protect her own skin.

She had lived long enough in the Celestial atmosphere to know full well what exquisite torture would fall to her share did she betray Sam Loo. She had seen a little of such things, and had no desire to experience them herself, though she was ever ready to lend a hand when some helpless victim was the subject.

Did Blake reveal his knowledge of English— and such revelation would be necessary did he attempt to bribe her—he knew that she would make off post-haste to tell Rymer. While on board ship it was her policy to curry favour with the official who held her comfort in his hands. For these reasons Blake felt that a waiting game was the only thing.

This plan, he imagined, would be Rymer's as well. He had been turned down too hard by Yvonne to make another attempt without devising some fresh mode of attack, and the very fact that he felt he held her at his mercy would tend to make him more confident as to the ultimate success of his efforts.

In this way the days passed with monotonous regularity. Every night when he retired, and every morning when he rose Blake moved across the cabin and struck the partition one light blow.

It was a signal to Yvonne that he was near her and watching, and though she seldom dared to reply to it he knew it would tend to comfort her.

For as the days passed it was a foregone conclusion that black despondency would assail her when she realised to the full the dangers by which she was surrounded.

New Year's Day passed without incident, but on the following day Blake achieved another step in his efforts which caused him considerable satisfaction.

For some reason or other, which Blake was inclined to put down to the work of the old woman, he had never been allowed on deck in the morning since his first day out. He had been compelled to go up in the afternoon with the other Celestials, and as a consequence he had not caught a single glimpse of Yvonne since her interview with Rymer.

To be ready for any opportunity of communication which might occur Blake had spent some time in the solitude of his quarters writing a note on cigarette paper. Anything larger would be extremely difficult to pass, and as he had not a little to say it had been most difficult to get it all in the small space at his command. He had persevered, however, and the result was a fairly decipherable note.

This is what he had written:

"On no account make a move of any description. Your game's a passive one. Rymer did not exaggerate danger into which you have come. Foolish girl to do so. Rymer may make no move until just before landing—if then. If he does, hold him off in some way. I am planning day and night. Leave everything to me, and when it is time to move you will hear from me. Fleur-de-Lys following. Important: In some way must manage get Sacred Sphere to me. It will be tremendous danger to you if plans fail at present. Do this without fail, but be careful. Keep up your courage. Will rescue you eventually.—S. B."

This note he had carried with him day and night, ready, if the chance came, to pass it to Yvonne. And how that chance did come was owing to Rymer's over-indulgence in celebration of the New Year's festivities.

On the morning after, Blake's breakfast was brought by the big Martinique negro. So regularly had Rymer appeared with his meals that Blake imagined immediately something must be wrong.

As he ate the coarse food he began to reflect. He remembered that Rymer had always had a weakness for the rich things of life, and if Captain Jonas Pettigrew had by any chance put in a stock of spirits it was just possible the New Year had been ushered in by much hilarity in the after part of the ship.

It happened that Jonas Pettigrew was just enough of a New Englander to attach great importance to that day, and for the occasion he had brought to light, not only spirits, but wine, which on ordinary occasions his frugal nature would not permit him to dispense freely.

It had been exactly as Blake thought, and when the morning wore on without any signs of the second mate he decided to risk a journey to the deck.

With this idea in mind, he softly opened his door and looked out. Not a soul was about. He gave a glance at Yvonne's door, then turned and made his way, not towards the forward hatch, but in the direction of amidships, where the narrow companionway which Yvonne used was situated.

He had no idea if Yvonne and the old woman were yet gone on deck. Things had been quiet for some time in their quarters, and he thought it just possible they were. He reached the companion without seeing anybody, but as his head emerged above the level of the deck he saw Yvonne coming towards him, her features heavily veiled as usual, and with her was the old woman.

Naturally, she would have no idea which Celestial was Blake, and he dared not risk a meaning look under the eagle eyes of the old hag. Instead, he turned his head away indifferently, and stepped to one side as they approached. But the side to which he stepped was the side on which Yvonne walked, and as her hand swung past as she went by Blake's fingers touched it for the barest fraction of a moment.

When he did so his hand had held the tiny note; when it came away it was empty. Yvonne's quick wit had helped her in that moment, for the slightest hesitation or bungling on her part would have caused failure, if not exposure.

As they disappeared along the deck Blake made his way to the side, and stood gazing over for several minutes; then he turned and made his way back to his quarters. That was the step which he had achieved.

That afternoon he took his exercise as usual. He went up, ate, and the short winter day was fast closing in when he started to descend. Before he did so he cast his eyes around the cold grey horizon, and far astern he saw a black cloud of smoke. He wondered if it might be the Fleur-de-Lys, and it happened that it was.

And Yvonne! What of her since the morning she had received the astounding intelligence that Blake himself was on board, the Eastern Queen?

Ever since Mother Peters had entered and discovered her crouching on the floor by the wall she had been watched incessantly. Even in the privacy of her own cabin she seemed to feel the eagle eye of that old wretch upon her. She could not make out when her jailer slept, unless it were that she possessed the canine faculty of sleeping with one eye open.

But not fifty nor a thousand Mother Peters could see into her heart or hear the song of gladness which it sang. The deadly oppressiveness which had begun to assail her, and the plain facts of the danger which had confronted her, seemed to melt away in the rush of confidence and love which overwhelmed her when she thought of the silent, unyielding force of the man so near.

Never while he lived would Blake know how she awakened early in the morning, lying with closed-eyes and throbbing pulses, waiting for the one stroke which would tell her he was there. And at night when she had retired, regardless of the eye of Mother Peters, she would surreptitiously pull from her throat the miniature which hung there, and when his nightly signal came she would press her warm lips to it and breathe ever so gently "Good-night!"

And it was this love which Dr. Huston Rymer desired.

It was only by the slimmest margin that Yvonne succeeded in getting the note which Blake thrust into her hand. She had, as he thought, no idea that the Celestial whom she had seen on deck the first day was in reality Blake.

At the same time, she knew he would seize the first opportunity which came of communicating with her. Consequently, from the moment she left her quarters until she returned she was on the watch for anything which might occur.

No opportunity occurred of reading the note until she had retired that night. Even then she made no attempt to do so until after Blake's signal, and on this night, as she had done only once or twice before, she risked a reply. It would tell him that she had received the note, and no matter what it contained would do exactly as he said.

Then carefully concealing it by her arm from the prying eyes of the old woman should she chance to be spying, she opened it up, and began to read the almost microscopic writing which covered it. When she had finished, she lay back and blew out her candle.

For a solid hour she remained steeped in thought. At the end of that time she had come to a decision as to how she should convey the Sacred Sphere to Blake.

Though she had passed with it so far without discovery it was only because she had not been kept in a state of coma by drug. If that had been the case, the old hag's sharp eyes would have detected it long since.

But after she reached America it was another matter. Through the underground channels there no risks would be taken, and the chances were if she were not kept in a complete state of unconsciousness she would, at least, be kept partially so, and in this condition her trinkets would be at the mercy of Mother Peters.

This conclusion arrived at, she rolled the cigarette paper up into a tiny ball and calmly swallowed it. That done she proceeded to do a curious thing. Slipping out of her bunk, she searched about the floor until she found one of the shoes she had worn during the day.

With that in her hand she returned to her bunk, and kneeling down rested the shoe, heel downwards, on the edge, then putting all her weight on the shoe she bore down heavily, until there was a sudden give. The shoe had come away in her hand, the heel had fallen into the bunk.

Yvonne laid the heel and the shoe on the floor, and slipping back into her bunk settled herself for sleep. The next part of her plan would not be put into operation until the morning.

It was before daybreak that she awoke, and lay as usual waiting for Blake's signal. Something must have stirred the detective earlier than usual this same morning, for his stroke sounded against the partition less than half an hour afterwards. Like lightning Yvonne was out of her bunk.

Picking up the shoe and heel, she bent down close to the wall and began to hammer boldly. At the second thump Mother Peters entered on the run, but Yvonne went on coolly, as though she did not exist. For once that cunning old hag was completely befooled.

She saw the slipper, the heel which had come off, and the kneeling girl hammering at them as though to fix them. What more natural? But she did not know that those same thumps were carefully calculated in the space of time between them, and that on the other side of the partition the Celestial Chen Foo was spelling out the words:

"M-y—p-i-l-l-o-w—"

Yvonne dared risk no more, and when Mother Peters approached and demanded the shoe she handed it over meekly. The old woman sent it to the carpenter to be fixed—proceeding which would naturally have occurred to anyone.

Two hours later, when Yvonne left her quarters for exercise on deck, she possessed one thing less than she had. That was the Sacred Sphere. It lay under the pillow on her bunk, and it remained to be seen if Blake would succeed in getting it.

In his cabin Blake had heard Yvonne's first tap. He was about to turn and light a cigarette, but when a second and then a third tap came he stood motionless. All he caught of the first word was the letter "y."

The word "pillow," however, he got perfectly, and it needed little deduction on his part to guess that the missing letter was "m." It meant that Yvonne had read the note, and had acted without loss of time.

It seemed an eternity before the listening detective heard the door of the adjoining cabins open and the swish swish of their skirts as Yvonne and Mother Peters passed on the way to the deck. Blake gave them time to reach the companion-way before he moved.

When he judged they had done so he noiselessly unlocked his door and looked out. There was nobody about. Stealthily he passed out and tiptoed along until he reached the next door. If Mother Peters had locked it all Yvonne's strategy and his caution would go for naught—for that day, at least. Unconsciously, he heaved a sigh of relief as the door yielded to his pressure. A moment later and he was inside.

Did chance bring Rymer or anyone else at that moment, his position would be as precarious as it had ever been in his long career. He touched the powerful automatic which was concealed beneath his jacket, and vowed grimly that if he were discovered he would get a few of the ship's company before they overcame him.

Instinct as well as the observations he had made told him Yvonne's cabin would be the inner one. To this he made his way at once, and pushed aside the half-open door. A familiar perfume met him as he did so, and even had he not known before he would have been certain now that Yvonne had lately occupied it.

Before him, against one wall, ranged her bunk, neatly made up.

At the upper end was a large pillow, the smooth appearance of which gave no hint of what might be underneath. Two strides took Blake to it.

With a quick thrust, he pushed his hand under the pillow, and his fingers closed on something hard and round enclosed in a soft chamois covering. It was the Sacred Sphere of the ancient Ming Dynasty. He smoothed the slightly rumpled pillow, and turned to make for the door.

Just as he reached it, and was about to pass into the outer cabin, a knock came at the outer door, followed by the turning of the handle. Blake stiffened, and stood behind the shelter of the narrow door. Had he, after all, grasped success only to have it snatched from his grasp? It certainly looked like it.

He heard the outer door open and a heavy step sound in the other cabin. Whoever it was, it was neither of the women. Then the footsteps approached the door behind which he was concealed.

Silently his hand slipped up under his jacket and gripped the butt of his revolver. As it did so, the hand and forearm of a man appeared around the edge of the door, the fingers gripping it as their owner stood and surveyed the cabin.

One glance showed the fingers and arm to be Rymer's. If he came six inches more nothing could avert discovery, and, from Blake's point of view, a premature settling of accounts between them. At that moment he heard a mutter.

"Must have gone up by the companion as I came down the ladder."

With that, Rymer's arm disappeared, and his footsteps sounded as he passed through the outer cabin and slammed the door. How little he dreamed how close he had been to Sexton Blake—and death! for had Blake and Rymer had a settling of accounts that day it would have been to the death.

Blake's fingers loosened their grip on his revolver, and he stole into the outer cabin.

"A close shave," he muttered. "He is sure to go up on deck to see if they are there, but he may return to see me, since he hasn't been about for a day. I'd better get into my cabin as soon as I can."

Softly he turned the handle of the door and slipped out. A moment later he was in his own cabin, and barely had he thrust the Sacred Sphere into an inner pocket, when there was a knock at the door.

It was Rymer.

From that day on Rymer's attentions to Yvonne and Blake were as unremitting as they had been during the first days of the journey. If he was weaving any new scheme in his mind which included Yvonne he kept it to himself, and beyond letting her feel how completely she lay at his mercy he left her alone.

As for Blake, he ate, exercised, and slept with maddening regularity. It was well he had communicated with Yvonne on the one slim chance which had offered, and that she in turn had lost no time in acting on his wishes; for from that day not a solitary chance presented itself for any communication between them.

Blake was kept to afternoon exercise, and beyond the morning and evening signal they neither heard nor saw anything of each other.

With that almost uncanny favour which Nature sometimes showers on evildoers, the Eastern Queen was given a fair wind clear across the Atlantic, and exactly nineteen days out of Cardiff, the blue coast of Nova Scotia appeared to the westward. That afternoon they rounded treacherous Cape Sable, and a little later lonely Seal Island was passed. Then they turned into the Bay of Fundy, and headed for the southern coast of New Brunswick.

Captain Jonas Pettigrew evidently had some reason for not laying his course direct for the port of St. John, for he made off a point to westward until first the Wolves and then the Island of Grand Manan appeared.

The latter, a crescent-shaped, lonely island inhabited by a handful of fishermen, came in sight just as night fell. The brilliant light on Southern Head, which rears itself at the very edge of gigantic cliffs against which the sea beats in wild fury, and about which the gulls wheel, shrieking with an almost human wail, shone out just as the waves grew leaden.

Far away at the other end twinkled the sister light on North Head, and a distant gleam showed where the outermost rampart of Campobello stood sentinel at the entrance to Passamaquoddy.

Little indeed had those barren coasts changed since the ancient red man stood and gazed in wonder at the unbelievable expanse of water with which the Great Spirit washed his doorstep.

With the lights of Grand Manan on her port bow, the Eastern Queen scudded along until she passed White Head; then the man at the wheel threw her over, and she headed up the Bay of Fundy, laying her course almost parallel with the near, but invisible, coast of New Brunswick.

All night she kept on this course; but as day broke over a grey, stormy sea, Rymer, who was on the poop, saw a black speck speeding towards them. It grew larger and larger, and through the flying spray, which curved outwards from her bow like lips of alabaster, he saw the slim, black shape of a powerful motor-boat.

Nearer and nearer she drew until within hailing distance. As a shout broke over the water. Captain Pettigrew and Kelly, the mate, appeared. Pettigrew waved his hand in reply, then turned to Rymer.

"We transship our cargo here. You had better have them brought on deck at once."

Rymer nodded curtly, and turned to go below. When Captain Jonas Pettigrew had explained to Rymer the workings of the underground system as far as he knew it, Rymer had seen a big complication ahead for him in the transshipping of the cargo in the Bay of Fundy.

It meant the removal of Yvonne from his immediate supervision, and though he had played a waiting game, he had by no means given up his intentions regarding her. Furthermore he was as determined as ever to get his fingers on the reward offered for the Lady Sybil, and though he might know all the theory of the underground system, he realised only too well that this would avail him not at all unless he personally could follow through the secret chambers in company with a cargo.

A wild idea entered his head to disguise himself as a Celestial and attempt to get through in this way, but second thoughts showed him the idea was ridiculous. His knowledge of the language— or lack of knowledge—was sufficient in itself to preclude any possibility of success on that score. And yet to make a false move now would be to spoil every one of his carefully laid plans.

During the long voyage he had given the matter very deep thought, and a plan had occurred to him which, could he carry it through, promised some seed of success. Consequently, he showed no signs of his inward perturbation as he went to do the captain's bidding.

In anticipation of soon landing, the main body of the Celestials had gathered together what bundles they possessed. As for Blake, he had not been on deck since the Island of Grand Manan had disappeared from view the previous evening, and though he could tell the vessel was "heaved to," he had no idea for what reason.

Things had been strangely silent in Yvonne's quarters, and a feeling of foreboding came over him as the silence continued. It was not until some time after Rymer had hauled him on deck that he discovered the reason.

He joined the other Celestials who stood lined up against the side for inspection and count. A furtive smile, almost broke through Blake's impassive features at the humour of the situation.

With Dr. Huxton Rymer as second mate on a ship which smuggled Chinese, with Yvonne a captive on the same ship, and with Blake accepted as one of the Celestials, it was a situation which appealed to the sense of humour of the latter.

Rymer showed how little he realised the true condition of things as he walked along the line, counting and making a cursory examination of each man as he passed. Blake was the last in the line, but evidently Rymer thought his daily inspection of the fortieth man sufficed, for he barely glanced at him.

This finished, a rope ladder was thrown over the side, and as Blake stood nearest he was the first to descend. It was then he saw the motorboat for the first time, and as he realised the meaning of it all he was for once in his life at a momentary loss what to do.

If Yvonne were still aboard the Eastern Queen it would indeed upset his plans to leave. Then he remembered the silence in her quarters and moved ahead. His deductions had led him correctly so far. He would not relinquish them now.

He leaped from the bottom of the ladder across to the deck of the motor-boat which swung alongside. A big cabin was placed forward, and into this a short, bearded individual motioned him. Blake descended the few steps which led into it, and as he gazed ahead through the semidarkness of the place, he saw, stretched out on a couch at the far end, the relaxed figure of a girl. Beside her was the old woman.

Only too plain now was the meaning of the silence in Yvonne's cabin. She had already been forced into unconsciousness by a drug, and in this state she would undoubtedly be kept for many days. No matter how willing she might be, she was now powerless to assist Blake in any plan he might devise for her rescue. From now on it was a lone hand for him.

The rest of the Celestials followed hard on his heels, and when the last man had entered, the rope holding the motor-boat to the brigantine was let go. The purr of the motor sounded as she drew away, and a moment later she had swung round, heading Blake knew not where.

It began to look as if he would have his work cut out to succeed in getting a message to the Fleur-de-Lys. He realised, however, that the motor-boat could not cruise for long in the Bay of Fundy with a cargo of Celestials on board. They must land some place soon, and as he never crossed a bridge until he came to it, Blake closed his eyes, and waited for the next step in the game.

So far, he had succeeded in taking two tricks. The third was now being played, but it remained to be seen whether Blake would win or lose it.

The day wore on, and about four in the afternoon another night began to shut in on them. It was deadly cold outside, for no more bleak stretch can well be found in the winter time than the storm-swept Bay of Fundy. A fire in the cabin made it fairly comfortable there, however, and thinly clad as were some of the Celestials, it was well this was so.

It was not until Blake judged it to be past six that the motor-boat showed any signs of slackening speed. First she slowed down to half speed, then the engine stopped altogether. A moment later a soft bump told Blake they had struck a mooring of some description.

Just then the man with the beard poked his head into the cabin, and said in fluent Chinese:

"Look here, you fellows, we have docked, and unless you want to be caught, let me tell you to do exactly as you are told. You will come out one by one and land. A man on the wharf will point out where you are to go, and as you value your lives go straight there. You will have to stay in the place two days. The vessel which takes you on the next part of your journey is two days late. Now then, old woman, give me your charge. I will go first, and take her."

He moved along as he spoke, and picked up Yvonne as though she were a child; then he made his way out, and disappeared in the darkness, followed by Mother Peters. Blake was at the door in two strides, intercepting another man who had started to go out.

Pushing past, he gained the deck, and found they were moored beside an old wharf in a harbour of some sort. All around the shore were strings of lights, and behind ranged a city.

At first Blake was confused, but as he got his location more perfectly he recognised the sheet of water before him. They were moored in St. John Harbour, the great winter port of Canada.

This much he discovered, but no more. A gruff voice to his left caused him to turn and start in the direction from which it came. He found himself stepping from the motor-boat across the side to a landing at the foot of a flight of steps which led down from the top of the wharf.

A shadowy figure approached, and pointed upwards. Blake mounted at once, finding, as he did so, that the steps were treacherous and slippery from the frozen slime which covered them.

At the top another figure stepped forward, and pointed to a row of dark buildings at the head of the wharf. As Blake looked in that direction he saw a blotch some distance ahead also making in that direction. He knew it to be the man from the motor-boat with Yvonne in his arms, and old Mother Peters trotting along beside them.

Now, if at any time since he left Cardiff, was Blake free to escape. A few quick strides would have put him out of reach of the nearest of the agents of the System, and, as far as he could see, he was at liberty to traverse the full length of the dark wharf without being accompanied.

With a genuine parcel of "cargo" a guard is only necessary in order to protect them from their own mistakes, for the Celestial who is anxious to get into forbidden America is only too ready to trust himself to the care of the System until it finally lands him in the Chinese quarter of Boston, New York, or wherever he is booked to go.

Blake's hand insinuated itself up under his jacket, and his fingers closed on the butt of his revolver. For a fleeting moment the idea came to him to make a dash, knock on the back of the head the man who carried Yvonne, tear her from his grasp, and make his escape.

Had Yvonne been conscious, such a proceeding would have stood some chance of success; but he realised the old woman's cries would bring the rest of the agents down on him hotfoot.

If it had been nearer the city, where police and immigration officials might be about, even then he would have attempted it, but so lonely was the spot at which they had landed he knew full-well it was given over to the mercies of the night-prowlers of the harbour front.

By this time he was half way up the wharf, and the sudden disappearance of the party ahead through the open doorway of one of the buildings put an end to any thoughts of an attempt to escape.

He quickened his pace somewhat, for if they were to be hidden in the same house, he wished if possible to be near Yvonne. Then he stood some chance of knowing whether she would make one of the party which would leave in two days' time.

He found a man standing by the door, and as Blake approached the fellow scrutinised the detective's features. Satisfied that he was one of the cargo, he pressed a button. A moment later the door swung open, and Blake was pushed through into a dark passage-way.

A hand came out of the darkness and led him along to the foot of a flight of stairs. Up this he was conducted, until at the top a door was reached.

On being opened, it proved to be a big room containing no furniture, except a long table in the centre and about two score of mattresses ranged on the floor against the wall. The door closed behind him, and the sound of retreating footsteps told him his guide had departed to bring along the next man.

Blake made a quick examination of the room and windows, for he realised he must make a move soon in order to communicate with the party in the Flour-de-Lys. There were no doors beyond the one by which he had entered. A glance at the windows showed them to be closed on the outside by heavy shutters. A move to open one of them would soon attract attention, and moreover he doubted if it would be of any use, for from the location of the room he judged it to look out on the rear of the house itself.

As he heard footsteps again approaching up the stairs, he turned away and threw himself down on one of the mattresses, murmuring:

"Well, about the only thing I seem to have achieved to-day is to discover the name of the motor-boat—the 'Spitfire.' That is not much, but if she is the one which takes us away from here, it may be the card which will win the trick. Time will tell."

The door opened just then to admit another Celestial, and Blake nonchalantly lighted a cigarette. They began to arrive thick and fast now, and in less than half an hour the whole forty had been safely lodged in the big room.

The next day and night passed even more monotonously than

those on board ship. During the day, Blake amused himself by writing a short code message to Tinker on cigarette paper, and from one of the other Celestials he got an envelope. Enclosing the note in the envelope, he sealed it, and wrote on the outside:

"Yacht Fleur-de-Lys. In Port. Urgent."

And underneath:

"Finder keep money, but please take note to above address at once. It is important."

Then taking a piece of paper from one of the bundles of another Celestial, he wrapped it about the envelope, at the same time enclosing two English sovereigns. That done he tucked it beneath his jacket to await a chance.

On the evening of the second day the bearded individual from the boat appeared, and spoke in Chinese to the "cargo."

"Half of you will have to remain here another two weeks," he said curtly. "Half will get ready to leave to-night. You will be taken aboard inside an hour; but we don't leave the harbour until daylight. I have brought forty slips of paper with me. In order that you may not squabble over who is to leave and who is to stay, I have left twenty-one slips blank and the other nineteen I have marked with a cross. Those who draw marked slips go; those who draw blanks remain. Now, then, look lively!"

Blake listened in consternation to this unexpected denouement. Since the party was to be divided up into two and sent at different times, it was obvious that they were to be sent directly into the channel which would carry them across the American border. The question was, would Yvonne be sent with the first party, or the second?

If with the first, it was essential that Blake should leave with it also; if the second, then to leave now would cause him to lose sight of her entirely, and Heaven only knew what developments might take place before he again discovered her whereabouts. But something must be decided, and decided quickly.

Suddenly he remembered that instead of the "cargo" being halved, it had been divided into unequal parties, one of nineteen and the other of twenty-one. He argued from this that the smaller party, which was to go first, must be smaller for the reason that the extra facilities were required in another direction.

That being so, who more likely than Yvonne and the old woman?

Besides, since she was being kept in a state of unconsciousness it was natural that they should dispose of her as quickly as possible.

This conclusion reached, Blake moved forward with the others to draw his slip, determined if he drew a blank to buy or, that failing, to take by force a marked slip from one of the lucky ones. He was determined, by hook or by crook, to go with the first party.

Thrusting his hand in amongst the forest of yellow fingers which stretched out eagerly for a slip, Blake grasped one and drew it out. A wave of disappointment swept over him as he saw the side towards him was blank. Quickly he turned it over, and heaved a sigh of relief as there before him he saw a rude pencilled cross.

Fortune was with him, so far. He was to go.

As soon as the draw was over, the man from the boat marshalled up the nineteen and started them for the wharf one by one. Blake squeezed into a middle place, for he judged those at the front and rear would be more closely guarded than those between, who would be trusted to follow the leaders. The bearded man himself would probably bring up the rear.

At intervals of a minute they were started off, and eight were gone before it was Blake's turn. As the man in charge signed to him he passed through the door and down the stairs. A man there let him out and pointed towards the wharf. Blake bent his head and started over the road.

Half way across his arm shot up under his jacket, and he drew out the note he had written. Without slackening his pace in the slightest degree he hurled it from him through the darkness. A soft thud somewhere behind told him it had landed on the pavement.

He realised to the full the risk he had run; but it was his only chance of communicating with the Fleur-de-Lys, and must be taken. The note might even now fall into the hands of one of the agents of the System, or into the possession of some unscrupulous dock loafer.

In either event, the money would be kept, but the note stood little chance of being delivered. However, that had to be risked.

Two minutes later Blake descended the steps and crossed to the motor-boat, which he saw was the same by which he had come. The other eight men were already in the cabin, and he took his place beside them.

A curtain now concealed the couch at the upper end of the cabin, but the bottom of a woman's skirt which could be seen sticking out told him old Mother Peters was there—and that meant Yvonne. Blake began to wonder if, after all, he might not swing the third trick in the game.

Hour after hour passed, and still they sat there silently waiting for day to appear. After what seemed an eternity of time, the first grey of dawn began to spread across the winter morning, and with it came the tramping of feet on deck. Low voices as though in argument followed, and Blake, who sat somewhat near the door, shifted his position in order to hear.

They were speaking in English, and evidently cared little whether they were overheard by the Celestials, or not. One voice Blake recognised as that of the bearded individual; the other was—Rymer's!

At last the latter had moved, and as he listened Blake knew he was lying to the other man.

"I tell you Pettigrew says I'm to go through with them," he said. "I have special business to put through at the other end, and besides, he thinks I should keep an eye on the cargo."

"Well," grunted the other, "this is the first time Captain Jonas Pettigrew has ever taken such a fatherly interest in the cargo after it has left his hands, but I suppose it is all right."

"If you have any doubts on the matter, send and ask him," bluffed Rymer boldly.

"By ginger! I would if I didn't want to get away at once," responded the other coolly. "However, stay if you want to."

They moved away at that point, and Blake heard no more. He had heard sufficient, however, to tell him that Rymer had by no means given up his intentions regarding Yvonne, nor his determination to trace through the channels of the underground system the whereabouts of the missing Lady Sybil.

He had deserted the Eastern Queen, and no doubt in a few hours Captain Jonas Pettigrew would be scouring the city for his missing second mate.

Five minutes later the purr of the motor sounded; the boat slipped away from the wharf, and they began moving through the icy water of the harbour on the outflowing tide, heading for the bay beyond.

●　　　●　　　　●　　　　●　　　　●

Just before dawn appeared that same morning, a heavy brewer's cart drew up at the head of a broad quay farther up towards the city, at which a slim, graceful-looking yacht lay moored. The driver tied his reins about the whip stock, and swinging over the wheel made his way along the quay. He drew up as he reached the gangway of the yacht and, opening his mouth, emitted a hoarse hail.

"Floor-du-Liz ahoy!" he shouted.

The bow watchman on the yacht came to the side and looked over.

"Ahoy, yourself!" he said.

"I've got a letter for you," called the carter. "Shall I bring it aboard?"

"Sure thing, old son! Just waltz up the gangway. I'll call the skipper."

The man on the quay lumbered up the gangway, and stood waiting. A moment later a sailor appeared and led him to the chart-room, where sat Captain Vaughan in pyjamas and dressing-gown.

The man handed the letter over.

"I was comin' along by the docks about an hour ago on my way to the stables," he said. "I kicked something on the pavement, and lookin' down I saw a packet. I opened it, and found that note and two gold pieces wrapped up. Well, I put the gold in my pocket. You can see on the envelope that it said to do so. As soon as I got my horses hitched up I drove along here with it."

While he had been speaking, Captain Vaughan tore open the envelope and glanced with knitted brows at the writing it contained. Suddenly he turned to the sailor.

"Have Master Tinker come here at once. Also call Mr. Kennedy and Mr. Graves."

The sailor hurried away, and in less than five minutes Tinker was there. Captain Vaughan thrust the paper over to him.

"I can't read this, my lad. Is it in code?"

Tinker took the paper and glanced at it eagerly.

"Yes, yes!" he said quickly. "It is from the guv'nor, and as plain to me as English. Who brought it?"

The captain jerked his hand in the direction of the carter.

Tinker turned to him:

"Where did you pick this up?"

"About half a mile down the docks, just opposite the old Colonial Wharf."

"Do you know a motor-boat here called the Spitfire?"

"I ought to, seein' as she lays at the Colonial Wharf, and I pass her every mornin' and evenin'."

"Good!"

As he spoke, Tinker thrust his hand in his pocket and drew out a sovereign.

"Here you are for your trouble. You needn't wait any longer."

The man took the gold, and tipping his cap awkwardly lumbered out, evidently more than pleased with his day's beginning.

As soon, as he was gone, Tinker spread the paper out on the table. At the moment Kennedy and Graves appeared, and stood just inside the door as they heard the lad's voice.

"This captain, is what it says:

"'Arrived and held in house opposite some old wharf. Transshipping in bay to motor-boat Spitfire, and brought here by her. Leave on Thursday or Friday by her. Imagine during hours of darkness or early dawn. Watch her and follow in Fleur-de-Lys. If we get into American waters, tell Kennedy to strike. We may be transshipped again. If so follow. And in any event move in American waters, but not before. Don't know that this will reach you, but am taking a chance. If hear nothing from you will try to communicate later. Yvonne well so far. Dr. Huxton Rymer one of the gang. Tell Kennedy thirty-nine Celestials besides me in the cargo. We must bag the lot.—S. B.'"

Twenty minutes later the Fleur-de-Lys slipped her moorings and headed for the Bay of Fundy under full steam.

With a ringing cheer Blake led the sailors from the "Fleur-de-Lys" to the attack.

THOUGH, it was well-nigh a month since the great Christmas Eve storm had swept across Canada, the surroundings of the little shack which bore the sign "Looey Sing, Laundry and General Stores" showed little change.

Perhaps the snow was a little deeper, and the drift-piled road had long ago been beaten into a hard, slippery track by the sleighs of the farmers.

Now it looked like a discoloured ribbon winding over a mantle of virgin white, the purity of which stood out startlingly against the emerald edging of fir and spruce.

Though the cold was not abated, and each night showed the thermometer down to twenty degrees or more below zero, the river was icebound no more. Great, powerful icebreakers had come up and ploughed a channel through it by which the small river steamers which supply the isolated fishing islands of Campobello and Deer Island could reach the wharves in the town above.

There they disgorged their cargoes of salt fish, frozen fish, and pickled herrings, which would soon go speeding north to Madawaska and Restigouche to the great lumber camps.

In return they loaded tier upon tier of flour in strong wooden barrels, cakes of tinned vegetables and meat, sacks of bran and shorts and middlings, molasses and pork and salt, not to mention the eternal barrels of pilot bread and cases of "candy," for the fisher children on those lonely islands have both a sweet tooth and a marvellous capacity for anything which pleases that quality of the palate.

Two miles below, in Looey Sing's shack, the same dingy stock still decorated—or encumbered—the front shop. The back room, where that uncommunicative Celestial passed his days and nights, showed not the slightest change, and, with Looey Sing himself sitting before the stove and smoking the eternal yellow cigarettes, it might have been back on Christmas Day, not nearly a month later.

As he had done on Christmas Eve, and, in fact, as he had done every day since, Looey Sing sat impassively until the short winter day drew to a close. But, unlike the days since that other one, he rose shortly after and proceeded to don his fur coat and cap. Replenishing the fire, he opened the rear door and stepped out into the clear, frosty

127

air.

Up above in a cold silver sky a chill moon sailed, bathing the snow-covered country in rays of cobalt. The hard facets of the encrusted snow glittered in the light like myriads of diamonds, throwing back the rays in countless points of light. The emerald woods had deepened in tone to that of the black fastnesses of the boundless ocean.

Somewhere in the distance a telegraph-wire sang, as wires do in Canada in the winter. In the woods a sharp, pistol-like report sounded from time to time as a weighted branch cracked in the frosty air.

It was a true winter night in New Brunswick, and even the apparently unemotional Celestial must have felt it, for he stood a moment gazing about him at the cold virginal glory of it all.

Taking a long breath of the biting air, he turned and crunched along a well-beaten path until he disappeared in the woods. He followed identically the same course which he had taken on Christmas Eve.

In near the edge of the bank a wide fringe of ice still clung, though now its once glittering surface was coated with snow. Further out many startling reports sounded as great stretches of ice would split in two, the dividing line which appeared being the only sign that this had occurred. The channel itself where the water ran free was a black band on a vast carpet of brilliance.

Following the bank of the river, Looey Sing kept on until he reached the little wooded cove where stood the boat-shed. There he proceeded to unlock the doors and busy himself at the winch. A moment later the boat rolled down the tiny track on its wheeled framework, and as the latter kept on into the black depths, the boat floated free on an inky bosom.

The purr of the engine broke out almost at once, and, as Looey Sing took the tiller, the boat headed down river in a wide sweep which brought it well out in the middle.

Over the same course went Looey Sing until he came abreast of the point guarding the entrance to Oak Bay. There he swung the tiller hard over, and a moment later the boat was driving along close to the shore, headed up the small bay.

No driving storm of hail and sleet blinded him this night. The moon threw into clear outline the timber-bordered shore where it broke against the tossing waters of the bay, which, fed by the salt spew from Passamaquoddy, defied the frost. Helped by the moon, he could see along for some distance, and a close observer might have noticed a barely perceptible flicker of the heavy lids as he peered ahead over the bows.

Long ere this the masthead light of the schooner should have shown. Certainly there was no mistake on the part of the Celestial. He had in his pocket a code telegram telling him the day and the hour at which the schooner would be anchored in the accustomed place. It had been sent from St. John just before the motor-boat Spitfire had left with the first batch of cargo.

Even in stormy weather connections had never been missed before; and certainly the elements could not be the reason on this occasion, for a fair up-river wind had been blowing for three days. At the very latest, the schooner should have made the rendezvous by dark. And yet it was now a certainty that she was not in the bay.

The motor-boat had now reached the spot, and passed over it at slackening speed. Soon the engine stopped, and as she went ahead under her own impetus Looey Sing sat contemplating the expanse before him.

"I no undelstand," he muttered, as he turned and gazed astern. "Teleglam say she be here. She not here allee samee. Someting happen. I go down river see what. Allee samee, Looey Sing no likee."

Once more he carefully scrutinised the bay, but not the remotest sign of a barque of any description could he make out. As far as could be seen, he was alone on the cold bosom of the bay. Starting the engine again, he sent the boat around, and went back the way he had come.

When the flashing light on St. Croix Island appeared he laid the boat's head for the American side of the river. Reaching there, he again altered his course, and in the black shadow cast by the tree-covered Devil's Head he started down river on his search for the missing schooner.

    •   •   •   •   •

While Looey Sing was speeding along in his attempt to locate the schooner a startling denouement had taken place a few miles down, just off the lonely shore on the American side, in St. Andrew's Bay— the small basin of water which passes on the flow of the river to the gaping maw of Passamaquoddy.

It was, in fact, a culmination of the third trick of the game upon which Blake was engaged, and as yet the issue was not decided. Certainly, Blake little thought the deciding card was coming through the night in a motor-boat. But how the crisis came is only explained by going back to the moment when the Spitfire, with her illegal cargo on board, stole out of St. John Harbour on the wings of a misty dawn.

Though his note to the Fleur-de-Lys had been written before he had any idea as to what Rymer's next move was to be, on thinking things over, Blake felt satisfied that, even had he known, he would not have altered the wording of it.

On the contrary, he felt that Rymer's appearance on the scene was a satisfactory point, for it meant one more loose thread gathered in. And certainly the skein was already sufficiently tangled.

Had he only known if his note was destined to reach the Fleur-de-Lys, he would have felt that his feet were on firmer ground than they were.

As it was, he had to go ahead as he would were the whole game to be played out by himself alone; and did the others turn up, then, if the issue by any chance hung in the balance, their arrival might turn the scale.

Reconstructing the line of thought he calculated Rymer would follow, and in view of the tenacity of purpose he knew that gentleman to possess, it was not hard for him to read the meaning of Rymer's coming.

Once she was clear of the harbour the Spitfire tore on down the Bay of Fundy, keeping in sight of the coast. It was a rocky outline in the winter-time at best, though in summer no more glorious fancy of Nature can be found than the zephyr-kissed shores of New Brunswick. From the few glimpses he caught of the shore through the cabin window Blake judged they were doing about twelve knots, and he was not far wrong.

All day the boat kept up this pace, and all day the Celestials sat in the stuffy cabin, ignorant of the next step in their long underground journey, but confident in the power of the men in charge to eventually land them where they desired to go. It was not until late afternoon that the boat's speed showed signs of slacking, and all hands moved with an unconscious air of relief. Even the impassive Celestial can feel the deadly drag of monotony.

It was evident that the schooner to which the bearded man had said they would be transshipped was in sight, and had there been any doubt in the matter, a loud hail on the deck of the Spitfire put it to rout.

An answering hail from over the water sounded faintly, and the motor started again as the Spitfire was headed in that direction. Five minutes later the cabin window on the port side was overshadowed, and a soft bump told Blake it was the side of the schooner. The man with the beard thrust his head into the cabin almost immediately.

"Look alive!" he ordered. "One at a time, and don't waste any time about it. There is smoke astern. It is probably a steamer coming up."

The Celestial nearest the door lost no time in acting, and the rest followed him hot-foot. Blake passed out last, and as he did so he saw Rymer behind him, bearing Yvonne in his arms. Evidently old Mother Peters had swallowed his bluff, as had the bearded individual.

Blake, being the last out, was still on the ladder which led over the side of the schooner when he heard Rymer's voice beneath him. Turning, he looked down, and saw the other was signing for him to take Yvonne and pass her over. Throwing one leg over the side, in order to steady himself, Blake leaned down, and held out his arms.

As Yvonne was placed in them and he felt the warmth of her relaxed body, a great wave of weakness swept over him, and for a moment he swayed; it was followed by a flood of rage at the whole cursed work of the System, and never in his life had Sexton Blake been nearer losing command of his temper than at that moment. He was beginning to realise that Yvonne's danger had struck a deeper chord than he imagined.

He held her very gently until Rymer reached the deck, though something at least of what he felt must have shown in his eyes, for as he took Yvonne, Rymer looked at Blake, and shivered slightly as he did so.

Had Blake been able to see his own eyes at that moment he would have understood the reason. He had veiled them so quickly, however, that Rymer began to feel uncertain whether or not the expression he had seen there was his own imagination. But, from time to time, he looked at the silent Celestial with a curious glance, and resolved that in future he would keep Chen Foo at a distance from Yvonne.

As soon as the "cargo" was all aboard and sent below, the Spitfire drew away and headed back for St. John. Then, as night closed down the schooner, which, by the way, was the same one which had borne a cargo to Looey Sing on Christmas Eve, took advantage of what breeze there was and laid her course for the mouth of the St. Croix River.

About an hour later a row of lights showed on the starboard side. It was the steamer, the smoke of which had been seen astern some time before, and in the glow of the electric bulbs Blake, who was leaning over the side, thought he recognised the slim lines of the Fleur-de-Lys.

For a moment he was puzzled as to why she should pass them, supposing it was she. Then he remembered that in his note he had told Kennedy to strike if they got into American waters. To do that the yacht would have to be authorised by the Government officials on the American side.

This meant that before striking the Fleur-de-Lys must make an American port in order to get the necessary papers of authorisation. In that was explained her reason for passing them, and, if it were she, there was no doubt but she was running for Eastport, that coast city of fish warehouses and sardine factories, which is situated at the very mouth of the St. Croix and which the schooner herself must pass before entering the river.

About seven the following morning the schooner passed through the channel between Deer Island and Campobello, and, coming away in a wide track to windward, headed up the river. The wind, which was fair, began to ease, and the outrunning tide meeting the waters of the bay, combined to make her progress slower.

However, with a moderate run, she should make her rendezvous, and, from the suppressed air of relief which rested on the lantern-jawed captain, Blake judged he hoped to do so.

As they passed Eastport, off to the left, he scanned the long line of wharves with an eagle eye. There were small river steamers moored there as well as a couple of big outside boats which traded between Eastport, St. John, and the larger port of Boston. Intermixed was a medley of sardine boats, some auxiliaries, and a host of open motor-boats, to say nothing of several schooners whose bare spars looked like a naked forest.

At first he could see no signs of the graceful lines of the yacht; but as the schooner shifted her course he caught sight of a white yacht moored at a short wharf below the Custom House. It was the Fleur-de-Lys, and he knew now his note had been delivered.

Slowly the shore passed until the schooner nosed the waters of St. Andrew's Bay. It was past noon now, for a good deal of time had been consumed in tacking. As a matter of fact, if the wind held, the captain figured on making St. Croix Island about dark, and the rendezvous a little later. This he usually contrived to do unless the weather forbade, for he had no fancy to heave to around the point in Oak Bay in daylight.

It was just after they had entered the bay and were making a long tack to starboard which carried them well over into the Canadian side of the river, that a cloud of black smoke appeared astern. Beneath it a shape rapidly came into view.

It began to overhaul them quickly, and as the captain of the schooner saw his next tack would take him fairly close to her, he issued orders that all Celestials who were on deck should go below at once.

He had no desire for any curious eyes to see the countenance of a Chinaman peering over the side of his ship, though in truth, the rapidly-falling night practically precluded any such possibility. Little did he dream of the identity of those on board the yacht.

So far as his next tack was concerned he was right. It carried him across into American waters, and as he got within hailing distance the lantern-jawed captain received a shock. On the bridge of the yacht stood two men in uniform. One of them had been leaning over the rail watching the schooner as she crept along over the imaginary line in the middle of the river which formed the boundary between the two countries. Then he curved his hands around his mouth, and shouted:

"Ahoy! What vessel is that?"

The captain of the schooner muttered a deep and fervent curse as he approached the side and spat into the water, then he raised his voice: "Schooner Southern Cross. Who are you?"

"Out of where?" came the voice of the man on the yacht, ignoring the counter-question.

"Out of Boston—bound for Red Beach."

"What is your cargo?"

"Coal."

"Heave to. I wish to come aboard."

"I'll do nothing of the sort! Who in blazes do you think you are?"

"I tell you to heave to, or I'll put a shot into you!"

"When you show me any reason why I should, then I will—not before! I want to make port tonight, and ain't goin' to heave to for anyone!"

A silence followed, then the voice again came:

"This is the yacht Fleur-de-Lys, temporarily in the service of the United States Immigration Department. I propose going aboard to inspect you and examine your papers. Will you heave to?"

Before replying, the captain of the schooner turned and spoke to the red-bearded mate, who had come on deck in haste.

"Have her put over hard," he said, in a low tone. "We'll run for the Canadian side."

The mate jumped to obey, and a moment later the schooner heeled as the booms came over, and she went off on a new tack. Almost immediately, there was a dull report astern, and a four-inch shell crashed through the rigging, taking a quantity of cordage with it.

The foresail came down with a ripping, tearing sound, and the foretop-sail flapped wildly as her stays gave. The captain leaped to the wheel, cursing, and shrieking out orders to the crew to cut away the damaged rigging, tried to keep her on her course. The yacht was now coming up hand-over-hand.

Seeing that the schooner did not stop, the gun again crashed out, and this time the foremast itself came down. At that the captain brought her round, and calling to his men, ordered them to arm themselves. The bow gun of the Fleur-de-Lys had done sufficient damage.

Blake had gone below with the rest of the Celestials, and though he could hear voices, which told him the yacht had drawn up and Kennedy was striking, he made no move until the first guns boomed out, then he acted.

Leaping to his feet, from the dark corner where he sat, he made for the door of the rough quarters in which the "cargo" had been put, and before any of the others could grasp his intention, he was outside. A moment only, and he had turned the key in the door, effectually stopping the participation of the Celestials for some time at least.

He made for the deck on the run, looking little like the heavy-lidded Celestial, Chen Foo. At the foot of the companion-way he stopped, but only long enough to draw his automatic; then he began taking the steps two at a time. On reaching the deck, a strange sight met his eyes.

The dying light was just sufficient to enable one to distinguish what was going on. The spars and sails of the schooner hung helplessly from aloft, and on deck a confused litter of sails, and ropes almost made the forward part impossible. Though a man still stuck to the wheel, she refused to answer her helm, and was drifting in slowly towards the American shore.

Almost the first person he saw was Rymer rushing forward, yelling like a madman, and brandishing a heavy Service revolver. The captain and mate were tossing over weapons of every description to the crew, who were massing behind the tumbled heap of cordage. In close was the yacht, drawing nearer every moment, and even as he looked she bumped. Then began a fight which, for swiftness of action, equals any tale out of the old stories of the Spanish Main.

Kennedy, Captain Vaughan, Tinker and Graves, leaped over the schooner's side, almost simultaneously. Hendricks, the mate, with Alec and the seasoned crew of the yacht, followed in a stream, armed with revolvers, cutlasses, and even belaying-pins. Almost ere their feet had touched the deck a heavy revolver fusillade met them from behind the heaped-up sails.

Blake made a running leap and hurled himself over a hatch to join the attacking party. His presence acted on them like a sharp spur, for as Tinker gave a hoarse cheer, the others took it up, and with Blake at their head, dashed forward. Two sailors had gone down under the first volley, and now a second volley came from behind the barricade. Some damage was done, and of the leaders, Hendricks was struck in the arm.

Until now the attacking party had held their fire, but at Blake's command they fired. It was a terrific volley which followed. Every revolver was one of heavy calibre, and seasoned as were the sailors, their aim was cool and steady.

A medley of shrieks and groans broke out on the other side of the barrier, but it was very evident that no surrender was intended, for several shots came zipping at the attacking party. That was the last volley from either side.

Blake and his followers were too close now for revolver work. With, a sharp order he clubbed his revolver, and, followed by the others, stormed the barricade. He made an odd-looking figure as he mounted over the heap of sails and cordage, risking everything to get into a hand-to-hand struggle. His bluejacket fluttered loosely, and his queue flapped behind him like a long braid. The sleepy look had left the eyes, however, and the cold fury in them was distinctly Anglo-Saxon.

For Blake was seething with a rage which had been steadily growing in him ever since he left Cardiff. Circumstances had made it necessary to hold it in check, but now that the crisis had come he gave it full reign. And Tinker, who had seen his master under all sorts of conditions, said afterwards that never before had he seen Blake fight as he did that night.

He swept over the barrier in a furious rush which defied opposition. Striking hard and straight with the heavy butt end of his revolver, he drove a couple of sailors to the deck and kept on, not knowing nor caring whether he was alone or whether the others were behind him.

He had one object in view, and that was Rymer. Nothing mattered now but to come to grips with his old enemy, and exact in one final settling, the revenge he felt was due to him.

At that moment one of the men who had been left aboard the Fleur-de-Lys switched on the searchlight, and trained it on the scene of the conflict. It lit up a strange sight indeed.

The captain of the schooner was lying doubled up in the scuppers with a bullet in his leg. Reddy, the mate, was wielding a belaying-pin, in a deadly struggle with Kennedy, the American Secret Service man. Tinker was cutting viciously with a short sabre at a big negro, who wielded a huge meat chopper with deadly intent. Hendricks had stopped long enough to bandage up his wounded arm, and with a sabre in his free hand, was driving a couple of sailors forward.

Alec and Captain Vaughan were in a tough melee with half a dozen Swedes at them, and the balance of the yacht's crew were fighting grimly in single combat. Each had picked his man, and with joy of battle in his eye, was fighting with sabre, revolver, belaying-pin, or in some cases bare fists.

Blake was occupied with a third, but straining every effort to reach Rymer, who, since the captain's fall, had assumed command.

He was standing back a bit, directing the efforts of his men. And yet he had taken no active part in the struggle, not because he feared to come to grips—for Rymer was never a coward—but because the attack had sent all his plans crashing to the ground, and his mind was working madly in an attempt to devise some means of averting the disaster which threatened.

It had been no small shock to him to see a Celestial leading the boarders, but not until the searchlight swept across the deck did he recognise the features of the man to whom he had handed Yvonne, and whose strange look on that occasion had caused him to shudder.

Even yet he had not realised the full truth, but as Blake's third man went down and he leaped towards Rymer, rapping:

"Come on, Rymer. You and I have a settling together!"

Then the light of recognition filled Rymer's eyes, and a soft curse broke from him.

Fool that he had been not to see through that disguise before.

It seemed that nothing could now prevent that long delayed clash; but something did, and that in the person of the wounded skipper, who, unseen by Blake, had rolled out of the scuppers and grasped his late passenger with all his strength about the ankles. Rushing as he was, Blake came down with a heavy crash, his head struck the deck with frightful force, his revolver flew into the scuppers, and for the time being he was non est.

Crawling forward, the skipper was about to deal him a further blow, when a great black shape shot through the night into the circle cast by the powerful searchlight, and before the terrified captain could help himself, he was rolling over and over in a death-struggle with Pedro's jaws at his throat.

The blow Blake had received had only partially stunned him, and in a few seconds he staggered to his feet. Well was it for the skipper that he did so, for only his command to Pedro prevented the great bloodhound from finishing his work.

He leaned against the side and passed his hand across his forehead. Before him the fight still raged, though with slackening vigour. Half of the schooner's crew lay about the deck, out of commission for the time being. The other half were being slowly driven forward to the fo'castle by the yacht's crew, though they stubbornly disputed every inch of the way. To all intents and purposes, however, it was a losing fight for them.

Of Rymer there was no sign. Even before Blake had fallen, Rymer had seen the day was lost, and, not even waiting to settle his old enemy, he had dashed below. A few minutes after he had regained consciousness, Blake saw the reason for Rymer's flight.

Coming out of the after hatch he saw a head, then a body, and finally a pair of legs. Another figure, and another, and another followed, until eighteen stood on the deck. Rymer had released the Celestials and turned them loose.

If the fight that had gone before was hot, that which followed beggars description. A few words from Rymer telling them they stood in danger of being captured after their long secret journey, had let loose a flood of savage rage which was deadly in its ferocity. Every one of them bore knives, and as the last reached the deck they tore along forward, shrieking like maniacs.

Only those who have witnessed the sight know the intense ferocity of a Celestial when running amok. Now, not only was there one, but eighteen, every one of whom had a knife in his hand and murder in his heart. Had Blake needed anything to clear his dazed senses that sight was sufficient.

With a swift motion he bent and reached his revolver out of the scuppers; then, levelling it, he began to send a hail of lead into the onrushing Celestials which succeeded in sending three of them to the deck, but did not stop the rest.

He gave a loud shout to warn the others, and, clubbing his revolver, stood ready to receive the attack. In a moment it was upon him. To this day Blake could not tell you exactly what happened from that on.

From the moment he found himself in a sea of yellow faces, with a dozen knives flashing in the rays of the search-light, he lost all count of detail and time. The berserker rage again seized him, and he fought with the fury of a madman.

A fleeting glimpse of a white face close to him told him that at least some of the yacht's party had seen the rush and had turned to meet it. Blow after blow he sent crashing straight into the yellow faces before him.

Man after man had gone down, but if he himself was wounded he did not yet feel it. His blue jacket was slashed to ribbons where the knives had ripped it; both his arms were bare to the shoulders, and his sleeves lay on the deck, clean cut away by the knives. But Blake heeded it not. A red mist suffused his eyes, and he only knew that he was fighting for his life.

Suddenly the press before him eased as others came to his assistance. He was aware that Hendricks on one side of him and Tinker on the other were swinging their sabres with deadly effect. In the momentary breathing spell he had he stood motionless, listening to a sound which came across the cold, frosty night air.

It was the throb of a motor growing louder each moment. Was it reinforcements from Eastport, or merely someone from the shore who had been attracted by the boom of the gun earlier in the struggle. In a few moments he was to know.

Even as he once more pressed forward and turned aside a slashing blow, the sound of the motor grew more distinct, and finally approached close to the schooner's side. It was Looey Sing, though Blake knew him not.

At almost the same moment Blake saw Rymer stagger down from the poop deck bearing a burden in his arms. Behind him came the old woman. In a glance Rymer took in the features of the new-comer, and approaching him, spoke rapidly. Blake saw the Celestial nod and turn back to the side.

In a second he read the meaning of Rymer's words. He had divined the identity of the Celestial, and had told him he had a precious burden which at any cost must be got away. As he realised this, Blake pressed forward savagely; but though he fought like ten men, he could not overcome the row of knives which kept slashing at him.

In less time than it takes to tell, Rymer was over the side with his burden. The old woman followed with surprising agility, and as she disappeared, Looey Sing turned and shouted something in Chinese to the Celestials. There were only about ten of them left in the fight, but as Looey Sing's hail reached them they swung like lightning and raced towards him. Blake, knowing Chinese as he did, understood that hail only too well. Looey Sing had shouted:

"Come quickly, pigs, if you would escape!" And they lost no time in going.

Their fallen comrades or the crew of the schooner mattered not if they could save their own skins and reach the golden land in safety.

With a shout, Blake tore after, followed by Hendricks, Tinker, Kennedy, and Alec. Graves, Captain Vaughan, and the sailors were still occupied with the crew of the schooner.

Had it not been for Rymer's anxiety to further his own plans, and his utter indifference to the fate of the Celestials, they might even then have got clear, for once they gained the boat they stood a good chance of getting away.

No sooner had Looey Sing reached the boat, however, than Rymer pushed off, the result being that the Celestials who flung themselves over the side landed not in the boat but in the icy water of the river.

Then it was that Blake and his companions, who had followed to deal out punishment, perforce had to turn to and take active measures to save the floundering beings in the water, which had already chilled them to the bone, and at the same time driven all the fight out of them.

As for Looey Sing, when he saw what had happened, he bent without the slightest haste and started the motor. A moment later it shot away from the side and headed at full speed up river, its occupants utterly indifferent to the struggling men in the water.

Blake cursed silently and redoubled his energies in order to lose no time. One by one the dripping Celestials were dragged aboard and sent to find their way to the cook's galley, where a fire burned.

As soon as the last was safe, Blake hurried forward, to find that the desertion of the Celestials and the fall of the mate had broken the last thread of resistance of the crew of the schooner. Already Captain Vaughan had driven them into the fo'castle and locked them in.

As soon as he got within hearing, Blake spoke quickly:

"Captain Vaughan, we must cast off at once. A motor-boat has come alongside and taken off Rymer. With him is Yvonne."

The captain, swung quickly, and rapped out an order to Hendricks.

"Mr. Hendricks," he said, "take six men and keep them aboard as a prize crew. Lock the Celestials in the cook's galley, and keep the crew in the fo'castle. Have your men cut away the wreckage, and make back to Eastport as best you can."

Then he turned to Blake.

"All ready, Mr. Blake. We will board that yacht, and, if human power can accomplish it, we will overtake that motor-boat."

At that moment Kennedy and Tinker came rushing up, with Pedro loping along behind them. They asked no questions, for well they knew Blake's intention as he sprang over the side of the Fleur-de-Lys. They followed hot-foot with those of the yacht's crew who were to go after them also.

It took very few minutes for those skilled hands to throw off the grappling-ropes and let the yacht drift away from the schooner. A moment later Captain Vaughan, who, with Blake, had gained the bridge, rang the engine-room telegraph, and the yacht began to gather way.

They were none too soon, either, for the American shore loomed perilously close. It was evident to those on the yacht that Hendricks would have his work cut out to get the wreckage cut away and make what sail he could, before the schooner grounded. And once aground, the outrushing tide would soon leave her high and dry, though not before the drifting ice-floes had done considerable damage to her sides.

The searchlight had been left trained on the schooner's deck in order that those left on board might have her light to work by. Now, however, Blake swung it around and sent its long, sword-like rays shooting along the bosom of the river.

Up, up, up they went, until they passed off the water and rested against a black point which stood out lonely and grim in the night. It was Joe's Point, which hides the bar at St. Andrew's from the view of navigators coming down the river. Not once had Blake picked out the motorboat.

Again he brought the light back to within a few hundred yards of the yacht, and again it went travelling over the water. Suddenly a black blotch appeared in the path of silver. It was moving at a rapid pace, and Blake needed no more to tell him it was the fleeing motor-boat containing Rymer, Yvonne, Mother Peters, and the unknown Chinaman who had come to their rescue so opportunely.

The schooner had now been left well behind, and the yacht was beginning to reach the full power of her engines. Swiftly though the motorboat was travelling, it could not escape the white rays which Blake held steadily on it.

In this fashion the chase went on for some little time, until at last the extreme end of Joe's Point entered the penumbra of the searchlight, and almost simultaneously the motor-boat disappeared behind it. For a time at least it must be a blind chase. The yacht forged on, keeping well out in the channel, for the St. Croix at night is a difficult passage for those who are familiar with every foot of it, let alone those to whom it is strange. Captain Vaughan had been up it twice, many years before; but in the lapse of time one's memory dulls on many trivial points of a tidal river, and at night, with an outrushing tide, it is these trivial points which may crop up and dislocate one's plans. They drew steadily nearer the point, and finally swept past at top speed.

Once more Blake sent the light forth, and far ahead, sticking to mid-channel, he picked up the motor-boat. Robbinston flashed by on the left, and in a few minutes they caught the gleam of the revolving light on St Croix Island. It was there that they again lost sight of their quarry, as the island hid it from view.

Captain Vaughan veered off to the American side in order to pass the island, and once again they picked up the motor-boat. It was flying straight up river, and had already left behind the point at the entrance to Oak Bay where the rendezvous was, at which the ill-fated schooner had failed to appear.

From that on it was an open chase until the old breakwater appeared. No sooner had it done so than Blake heard Captain Vaughan utter a low exclamation. He turned sharply.

"What is it, captain?"

"It has just occurred to me that with the tide more than half-ebb it is going to be mighty tricky getting through the Narrows just beyond the breakwater. There! With the light as it is now, you can see how the point on the Canadian side juts out and appears almost to touch the American shore."

"And there goes the motor-boat through," muttered Blake, as he held the light steady and followed with his eyes the configuration which the captain had pointed out.

Then aloud he said:

"Our quarry is gone through, Captain Vaughan. If it is a possibility, the Flour-de-Lys must follow. Remember your mistress is aboard that boat and at the mercy of Dr. Huxton Rymer if we fail to overtake it."

"You can count on my putting the yacht through if there is water enough to float her," returned the captain grimly. "Above the Narrows the river is wider and deeper, though in a hundred years the sawdust from the mills higher up has choked the channel considerably."

Both men turned in silence and stared ahead over the lit-up waters. The motor-boat was just disappearing behind the point which jutted out at the entrance to the Narrows, and a moment later she was lost to view.

Though it tried him sorely, Captain Vaughan rang half-speed as they passed the breakwater and entered the narrow water ahead. Through that cramped channel the tide rushed wickedly, carrying with it huge blocks of sharp-pointed ice which had broken off higher up. The Fleur-de-Lys nosed them unflinchingly, and a sigh of relief went up as she passed the first point in safety.

Slowly, with the dainty hesitation of a timid though determined maiden, she pushed on until the second bulge of the bank appeared. Now she hugged the curved bank on the American side, for there the water ran deepest. Ahead could be seen the red light of Bog Brook, telling of the danger, and behind them glimmered the Canadian lighthouse opposite the breakwater.

Every man on board leaned over and watched tensely the while the yacht forged ahead; then suddenly a deep, unconscious gasp ran over her from stem to stem its they felt a faint jar.

The Fleur-de-Lys had grounded in the Narrows, and not until the returning tide floated her could she hope to complete the passage.

For a single moment Blake raised his clenched hand and let it drop savagely on the rail of the bridge, the while he cursed silently. For one fleeting moment he contemplated taking a boat and, with half a dozen sailors at the oars, rowing after the motor-boat.

Then reason showed him how futile such a proceeding would be. No. For the moment he acknowledged himself beaten, and, with brooding eyes, he turned and went below, none attempting to speak to him.

With swift step Blake entered a cabin and shut the door. Drawing out a cigarette, he sat down and began to give his mind to the unfortunate denouement which had occurred. Certainly Rymer had so far played the winning card of that night's trick.

Not until the returning tide floated the Fleur-de-Lys did Sexton Blake move. It was now well past two, and the others, weary from the long fight, had turned in without undressing, to snatch a few hours' sleep. Simultaneously with the floating of the yacht they all appeared.

Blake was already on the bridge, and as Captain Vaughan came up he said curtly:

"Captain, we will go on through the Narrows until we reach the wider part ahead. Then we will turn and go back. I want you to break the record to Boston."

The captain looked at Blake in wonderment for a moment, for it was not like the detective to abandon a chase once he had set out upon it. He was too well-trained, however, to make any comment, and replied:

"All right, Mr. Blake. As soon as I get out of these treacherous Narrows you will see what she can do."

Wu Ling recognises Yvonne and Rymer.

WHEN Rymer had turned loose the cargo of Celestials, and with a few words had spurred them on to join in the slaughter on deck, he had sped along with no definite purpose in view to the cabin where Yvonne was kept.

His one idea, so far, was to create a scene of confusion on deck, under cover of which he might have an opportunity to turn events to his own advantage.

It was ever Rymer's policy to use a man or a system as long as it served his purpose, and when it had ceased to be useful to cast it aside as one does a dilapidated hat. It mattered not a jot to him that the captain and crew of the schooner might be overpowered and in the parlance of the country caught "with the goods on." They had served their purpose as far as he was concerned, and now he would, if possible, get clear.

For a bare moment he wondered if it would not be wiser to leave Yvonne and make use of the precious moments for his own protection. Then the dogged greed of the man came to the fore, and with it his undoubted love for Yvonne.

It was a strange combination of good and bad which contributed to the making of his decision; but had he needed anything to clinch it, the memory of the look in Blake's eyes as he called to his old enemy was sufficient.

He found Yvonne on a couch, unconscious, with old Mother Peters in maudlin terror on the floor. Rymer picked Yvonne up bodily and roughly kicked aside the old hag, who clutched his knees, begging him to save her.

"Get up, you old fool!" he snapped. "Nobody will trouble to hurt you. If you want to come with me follow close, but let me tell you I won't wait."

With that he hurried out, the old woman trotting along at his heels, muttering a wonderful mixture of prayers and curses and forebodings.

On his way to the deck Rymer formed his plans. Under cover of the fight he would lower a boat and get away, if possible. Before he could be overtaken he might reach the Canadian shore, and on that side of the line the yacht had no authority to carry on the fight.

He knew that Blake would follow, regardless of boundary lines, but he vowed grimly that once he gained the shelter of the timber on the shore it would take a strong force to land under the hail of lead with which he would meet them.

At that moment he had reached the deck, and there met Looey Sing, whose timely arrival had served as a marvellously fortunate occurrence for Rymer. The reader has seen what followed then, and how the chase progressed from the time Looey Sing sent the motor boat flying up the river until they passed safely through the Narrows, where the Fleur-de-Lys grounded.

It was only a short distance now to the wooded cove where Looey Sing kept his boat, and with unerring skill the Chinaman drove her in until she gently nosed the slip. Rymer lent a hand, and together the two worked the winch in silence until the boat rested on her wheeled framework in the shelter of the shed.

When Looey Sing had jerked the old woman out of the boat, and Rymer had taken Yvonne, the Celestial turned to the white man.

"You follow me," he said curtly. "We talkee when we get to my place."

He set off at a swift pace on the way to his shack followed by Rymer and the whimpering old woman. Once within its safety he bolted the door, and waved his companions to chairs. Rymer laid Yvonne on a couch, and turned to the fire with a sigh of relief.

For the moment, anyway, he was safe, and if he was any judge of the Celestial capacity for cunning, he thought he stood a good chance of getting entirely free, though to be sure, the Celestial must not be told all.

What had become of the yacht he had no idea. All he knew was that her searchlight had suddenly failed to follow their course, and on looking back just before entering the wooded cove, he had seen nothing of her.

As soon as he had divested himself of his fur coat and cap, Looey Sing lighted a yellow cigarette, and turned to Rymer.

"Now, then, we talkee!" he said.

Rymer nodded his head.

"Yes, I will tell you how everything happened."

Slowly he related to the Celestial how, as mate of the Eastern Queen, he had been in charge of the cargo of Celestials leaving Cardiff for St. John.

"After we transferred them," he went on, lying cheerfully, "Captain Pettigrew thought it best that one of us should personally accompany the girl. Sam Loo valued her highly, and as she is intended to be the wife of his Excellency Fu Kan, the Governor of Hamai, we could afford to take no risks. In fact, Mother Peters here bears a letter from Sam Loo to the governor himself."

Looey Sing turned quickly.

"Is that light?"

The old woman felt the safest course was the truth, and nodded.

"Yes, I have the letter. See!"

As she spoke she drew it out, and held it up. Looey Sing took it, and closely scanned the Chinese characters.

"It is the writing of Sam Loo," he said, handing it back. "Go on!"

Rymer did not answer for a moment. Now, if ever, was his opportunity to discover if the Lady Sybil had been shipped through the underground route; but he realised he was treading on very dangerous ground. A bold lie would be necessary to draw the truth from Looey Sing, but if his lie was clumsy, the Celestial would, at once become suspicious. However, he decided to risk it. He lighted a cigarette with an air of nonchalance, and went on.

"The reason we thought this the wisest plan was because another special bit of cargo which was sent through some time ago has not been heard from since."

Only Rymer knew how his heart hammered while he waited for Looey Sing's reply. At last it came.

"What bit of cargo you speak of?"

"It was sent from Cardiff about ten days before Christmas," answered Rymer. "The tramp steamer, Belle of 'Frisco, brought it out with a consignment of Chinese."

"That cargo went through my hands," rejoined Looey Sing curtly. "Nineteen men and a girl. The girl was sent through from here Christmas night with the others, and arrived safely in Boston. She may be there now, she may be in 'Frisco. I don't know."

Rymer breathed more easily as he realised his lie had gone down. Now he knew he was on the right track, and that the Lady Sybil had indeed gone by this route. If he could only play his cards rightly he would win out yet.

"Everything passed as usual," he said, returning to the explanation Looey Sing sought. "I joined the Spitfire the morning she left harbour. We had nineteen Celestials besides myself, the girl, and Mother Peters, here. We picked up the schooner in the bay, and transferred safely. The Spitfire then returned to St. John, and we made for the river.

"Nothing of a suspicious nature occurred until we got well into the river, and then the yacht you saw hailed us. When we refused to heave to she sent a couple of shots into us, and came alongside. You saw pretty well what followed."

"Then someone betray us," said Looey Sing. Rymer nodded.

"Yes, and I happen to be the only man who knows who it was."

"How that?"

"I will tell you. Just before we left Cardiff Sam Loo came aboard, and asked us to take one man extra, though we were full up then, and getting ready to leave. Well, we took him, and saw nothing suspicious about him. Sam Loo said he had just landed in England from Canton. He was one of the nineteen who left St. John in the Spitfire, and in some way he let the cat out of the bag to his friends, who must have followed us the whole of the way from England in the yacht. He is no more Celestial than I am, but is an Englishman, and his name is Sexton Blake. Did you ever hear of him?"

Looey Sing took one step across, and grasped Rymer by the arm.

"Is that the tluth?"

"Of course it's the truth."

"Then we move quick. I hear of Sexton Blake. I know of him velly well. He dangelous man."

"I know him, too," rejoined Rymer gloomily. He might have added: "I know the yacht, and all aboard her as well; and let me tell you, my friend, that the yacht and everything on her belongs to that girl lying on the couch."

He did not add this, however, for he had no intention of letting anyone but himself become aware of Yvonne's identity. All this time old Mother Peters had remained silent, her eyes darting from one to the other.

Looey Sing she accepted unquestioningly as part of the System to which Sam Loo belonged. Not yet, however, did she understand Rymer. From the very first she had mistrusted him, and yet not one solitary occurrence stuck out which by any chance she could call suspicious.

He had done as any other member of the System would have

done while on the Eastern Queen, and in the escape from the schooner he had done more, for not many of the members of the System would have risked a delay in order that she might come, too.

This generosity on Rymer's part awoke no gratitude in the breast of the old woman. She felt certain that he had some game of his own to further, and that had she have been in the way she would have been left behind. Which, as it happened, was the literal truth.

Confident though he was that he would eventually bend Yvonne to his will, Rymer had no fancy that her awakening should find that resourceful young woman without the old woman to care for her.

He felt he knew Yvonne well enough to be certain that no matter whether she had fallen into the hands of the System voluntarily, or accidentally—though since the fight he knew the former to be the case—and no matter how she might feel towards him, she was bound to be a little grateful that he had run some risk in order to bring the old woman, regardless of the fact that she owed her present position to him. And he was right, as later events were to prove.

Looey Sing had been in deep thought ever since Rymer had finished his explanation. Finally, he tossed away his cigarette, and turned to the other.

"You wait hele," he said. "I go to see if I get something to take us away to-night. If Sexton Blake on the tlail, the System she bust up. Anothel way must be found. It just happen the 'gleat head' is in Boston. I go thlough, too, and see him. Looey Sing, live hele no more. I must send teleglam to St. John, too. They bound to sealch thele pletty soon."

He shuffled away as he spoke, and entered the front shop. A moment later Rymer heard the tinkle of a telephone-bell, and Looey Sing's voice followed asking for a number. As soon as he got it, he asked who was speaking, and, evidently satisfied, said:

"You come now—to-night—instead to-mol-low night?"

Evidently the person at the other end said he would, for Looey Sing said "All light!" and rang off.

Then, he came back to the rear room, and began writing out a code message to warn the St. John agents.

"Me give that to deliver to send," he said as he folded it up. "He be hele in half an hour. You wait. Looey Sing go to pack up."

He disappeared into the front shop again, and Rymer drew up a chair before the fire, determined to let things take their course.

From the little Looey Sing had said, it was evident they were going through to Boston. If that turned out to be the case, it would suit him down to the ground, for he knew Boston thoroughly, and trusted to devise the next step in his own game when he reached there.

If he had only known the identity of the man to whom Looey Sing referred as the "gleat head," and who the Celestial said was now in Boston, Rymer would not have sat so confidently before the fire in the back room of Looey Sing's shop.

Instead, he would have taken Yvonne, and trusted himself to Fate, and risked Blake's vengeance rather than walk into the very jaws of the yellow dragon, as he was destined to do.

For the "gleat head" was none other than Prince Wu Ling, autocratic ruler of the powerful Brotherhood of the Yellow Beetle, prince of the royal blood of China, and one time claimant to the throne through his being the direct descendant of the last ruler of the Ming Dynasty.

Looey Sing returned to the room at intervals in order to get one or two things which he proposed to take with him. It was marvellous when he finished how little he really intended to take, and had Rymer only known it, almost half of his bundle was composed of banknotes of every denomination and condition. Looey Sing had profited exceedingly out of the "cargoes" handled by the underground system. A few minutes after the Celestial had finished a knock came at the front door. It was the driver of the covered sleigh which was to take them over the border. Rymer, at a sign from Looey Sing, picked up Yvonne, and made his way out.

The sleigh was a big, roomy affair, piled up inside with heavy fur rugs, and on the bottom were several foot-warmers. It was hardly less warm than Looey Sing's back-room, and when they were all in, a curtain at the back kept out prying eyes, and kept in the warmth.

Then a creak followed as the runners moved over the frosty road, and the shop of "Looey Sing, Laundryman and General Storekeeper" was left to the solitude of the winter night. Never again would the silent Celestial return, and until someone entered, the mice could hold high carnival in peace.

Up towards the town of St. Stephen went the driver. When he reached its outskirts he made a wide detour, which took them through a wooded road to a point beyond Milltown, the cotton town which adjoins St. Stephen. From there his course took him over a road, heavily lined with snow, and banked on either side by the tall spruce and fir, the cheerful birch and the lonely pine.

Almost at the very moment when Sexton Blake on board the Fleur-de-Lys made his way to the bridge to instruct Captain Vaughan to make for Boston, the sleigh containing Rymer and Yvonne crossed the line by way of the frozen river several miles up. At last they were in the States.

When the first grey of dawn appeared, the driver pulled into a lonely road leading to a more lonely looking farmhouse. There his passengers alighted, while the driver turned and started back for the Canadian side.

At the farmhouse the fugitives spent the day until night fell, when the farmer, who was one of the agents of the System, hitched up, and again they started.

In this fashion they continued their journey for over a week—driving all night and resting during the day, and thus was it that the cargoes of the underground system were put through to their destination.

Through the vast solitude of the Maine woods their course took them. They went by the loneliest roads in order to avoid the settlements and towns; and be it known that in Maine and New Brunswick such a proceeding is not difficult to accomplish. On from Maine through the snow-covered State of New Hampshire they passed until on the tenth day they reached Massachusetts.

At last they were on the final leg of their long journey, and soon, very soon, Rymer would need to play his next card.

If he had only known whom he was to find at his destination!

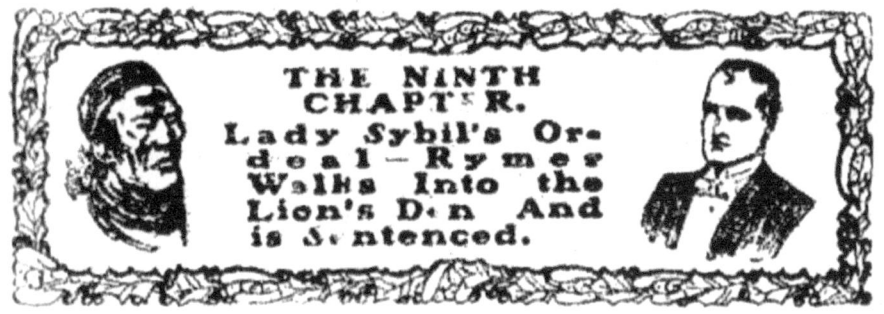

THE NINTH CHAPTER.
Lady Sybil's Ordeal—Rymer Walks Into the Lion's Den And is Sentenced.

THE city of Boston, in the State of Massachusetts, is the industrial centre of New England. Its population exceeds the half-million mark, and it is indisputably one of the greatest points of imports and exports in the United States.

If you ask a Bostonian what is Boston, he will gaze at you with a blank stare, and placidly inform you that Boston is the centre of culture in the United States and the hub of the universe.

Although the casual visitor would doubtless make some reservations regarding the latter statement, at least he would freely grant that the city was a marvellous hive of industry.

In itself, it is one of the most important railway centres in America, being the converging point of a myriad lines. Its woollen imports and exports are the largest of any port in the United States. Its manufactures are world renowned, for from it come boots and shoes, cotton goods of every description, confectionery, furs, hats, and a list of the needs and luxuries of man too numerous to mention.

All about it, like satellites about the mother planets, circle a host of smaller cities and towns, having their great woollen, cotton, and shoe factories, and making together one of the greatest manufacturing and industrial centres of the world.

Not only is Boston a great business port, but it is also the home of culture and education. Harvard, one of the greatest universities in the world, has its home there, and draws within its classic portals students from every part of the globe. Its museum of fine arts, its world-famed library, its technical school and medical colleges, all tend to contribute to the atmosphere of culture, and its public buildings are masterpieces of the builder's art.

There the first spark of the American Revolution was struck, and there was cradled the protest against slavery which gave rise to the American Civil War, dividing thousands of homes against themselves, and saturating the green fields of the South with the blood of her sons.

It is the birthplace of many eminent literary men and painters, statesmen and orators. The works of its poets are read in every home in the land, and its writers have by no means remained in the lower ranks of their craft.

And not only has Boston achieved distinction on these lines, but it has seen the springing into fame and power of many captains of industry, for more and more is commerce spreading out over the city.

The once aristocratic and exclusive residences of Beacon Hill and Back Bay in many cases now stand cheek by jowl with great retail shops. Their occupants, who find the proximity of trade an offence to their sense of the fitness of things, have sought refuge in Beacon Street and Commonwealth Avenue.

But if it is the city of industry and education, it is also a city of narrow streets and hidden vices, as is every other city in the world.

There, as in New York, Chicago, 'Frisco, and Montreal, is the inevitable Chinese quarter, and certainly the man who knows his way about can at times see things as unspeakable in the neighbourhood of Harrison Avenue and Kneeland Street, as he can see in the famous Mott Street district in New York, or in Little Lonsdale Street in Melbourne.

In a heavily-curtained, upstairs room, not a hundred miles from Kneeland Street, one cold, sleet-driven night in the early part of February, sat two men. Plainly furnished though it was, the room was a welcome retreat on such a night, for with the north-east wind whipping in off the bay in the winter time, no more cheerless place can well be found.

A table, a couch, three or four chairs, and a few really fine rugs, made up the furniture of the room. On the table was a nickel-plated oil-lamp, and sitting before some papers spread out beneath its glare were two Celestials.

One was stout and deliberate in his movements, though each gesture carried an air of deference in its train. Sexton Blake could have told you it was San, the faithful and indispensable lieutenant of Wu Ling. The other was the prince himself.

At present his eyes were bent on a telegraph form which lay on the top of several others. San's attitude was one awaiting his chief's pleasure. When he had read and re-read the telegram Wu Ling looked up, his deep, inscrutable eyes searching those of his lieutenant.

"It seems that destiny sports with us, San," he said slowly.

"Excellency, it is, as you see, the work of the man Blake."

"True, San, true. He it is who has thwarted many moves of mine. Never before has any man dared to pit himself against Wu Ling. And yet he still lives. San, the man Blake must go!"

"It is also the opinion of your most unworthy servant,

Excellency."

"It was a mistake to take the Lady Sybil," went on Wu Ling, musingly. "I should have taken other means to gain the information regarding her father's purpose in China, and what report he made to his own Government when he returned. She has been a complication, and, if I mistake not, it is her disappearance which put the man Blake on the track of the System I have so carefully organised. But since we have taken her, she will tell us what we wish, or pay the penalty.

"Looey Sing's message says he arrives tonight. He also says the old route is no more a secret to the authorities, and that he has been compelled to leave. Well, if the pig wishes to save his own skin what matters it? He has been faithful, and will prove valuable elsewhere. But the girl he says he is bringing—who is she? And the other man? He doesn't say. For that I must wait.

"He did well to send the warning to the agent in St. John, but he was too late. A thousand curses on the man Blake and his ancestors! Eight of my countrymen wounded in the fight, the captain and crew of the schooner beaten on their own ship, ten more captured, and twenty-one in St. John seized and deported. Thirty-nine men lost who would have gone to swell our forces here, and, worse than all, the secret route discovered! Pigs, dolts, fools! A thousand curses on them!

"To think that the man Blake came through as one of them, befooling even Sam Loo! He is getting old and careless. I will order him to China, and the price of his mistake, shall be his head. It is well, indeed, that I had the daughter of the English duke kept here until my arrival from 'Frisco."

For a few moments Wu Ling bent his head in thought; then again he spoke.

"San, have the girl brought in. I would speak with her. I shall then deal with her. Matters must be adjusted without delay before these stupid American pigs discover too much."

San rose at once, and, with a low bow, went out softly. Wu Ling sat perfectly motionless until he returned leading a girl garbed in English clothes.

Over her costume of pale pink, now soiled and crushed, was thrown a heavy coat of grey squirrel. Her features were now free from a veil, and though her eyes showed marks of the suffering through which she had passed, and her face showed a deadly pallor, she was still lovely to look upon. She seemed for all the world like some white flower which had been thrown into a choking bed of yellow poppies.

Wu Ling gazed at her with steady eyes, and as hers in turn rested on his, she made the first audible exclamation which had left her lips since she had awakened from drugged unconsciousness.

"Dr. Li-Fuang," she said, in low, vibrating tones. "So it is you whom I have to thank. Am I, then, in the city of Pekin? If you have the slightest vestige of feeling in you, tell me, I beg of you. Tell me where I am! Tell me what month, what week, what day it is! Tell me how long these creatures have kept me drugged, and tell me what is your purpose! Is it the custom, of Dr. Li-Fuang, the eminent Chinese statesman, to eat the salt of a foreign diplomat and return his hospitality by stealing his child?"

"Lady Sybil, you shall know all in good time, and rest assured no harm will come to you if you do as I demand. Then, and not before, you will know in what city you are. Then, and only then, will you know what month it is, what week, what day—yes, Lady Sybil, I will even tell you then what year it is!"

"Then it is the New Year!" she cried brokenly. "Oh, my father and mother will be mad with grief!"

"The sooner you do as you are asked, then the sooner will their grief be assuaged," replied Wu Ling suavely. "And, remember, Lady Sybil, your father is getting old!"

She swayed slightly upon her feet, and at a sign from Wu Ling, San gave her a chair.

"What is it you wish?" she asked in a whisper, her eyes wide with terror and suffering.

Wu Ling bent forward and fixed his eyes upon her.

"When you were in Pekin with your parents, you acted as secretary to your father, I think?"

She nodded, but made no audible reply.

"You also repulsed the attentions of Dr. Li-Fuang, or in other words, my attentions. Well, rest easy, my dear young lady, I never wanted to marry you; but I did want something else, and that is what you are going to give me to-night."

"What is it?"

"Information which you possess. Listen! Your father came to Pekin on a diplomatic mission which coincided with certain secret treaties which my Government made with Germany. He apparently came to make certain proposals regarding English trade with China, at least, so everyone thought but myself. I knew he came to investigate secretly our treaties with Germany. Not until he was gone without making any serious proposals did the others see that I had been right.

"While you were there, I made advances to you, thinking I might extract from you the information I needed. I saw I had made a mistake, and resolved to await my chance. That chance is come, and the price of your freedom is to tell me exactly what report your father made to the British Government on his return to England. If you tell me, I pledge you my word that you shall go free and unharmed. If you refuse—well, your life will be more terrible than in your wildest dreams you could conceive."

"In other words, you have come like a thief in the night, have torn me from my home, have brought me to some strange city, and have made the price of my freedom the betrayal of my father. You have made one mistake, Dr. Li-Fuang. You forget that you have English honour to deal with. You may take my life, but you cannot force me to betray my father. I refuse utterly!"

"Your life will not be forfeit," rejoined Wu Ling, in a tone of quietude which was far more impressive than any heated remark. "The dead rabbit feels nothing. Your punishment will be to keep you alive, and leave you at the mercy of my creatures. It will be to you a thousand times worse than death. You will know neither the city nor the town where you are kept. Your past life will be but a memory. You will be dead to your family and your friends.

"Your father and your mother are old. You are an only child, the pride and joy of their present, and a comfort for their declining years. All that will be over. To them you will be dead. To you the memory of them will be a spur of torture which alone will be sufficient to break your will and sear your soul.

"Think well what it means before you refuse, Lady Sybil. Think well of what you have left, and what the future will be. Now go! Think to-night, and in the morning let me have your answer. By it I shall be governed, and I tell you with all meaning that, if you refuse, your fate will be exactly what I have painted. Take her back. San."

San had to support the sobbing girl from the room, for the deadly menace in Wu Ling's tones had told her even more than the words themselves into what a living hell she would be thrust did she refuse to do his bidding.

But it meant betraying—perhaps politically ruining—her father, and she had too much of the ingrained English notion of honour in her to sacrifice another in order to save herself. And yet what a price!

Certainly, as she was led back to the charge of the woman who guarded her, she had a problem to settle that night which was as torturing to decide as any young girl torn from a sheltered home had ever grappled with.

How little we really grasp the idea of the thousands of miserable problems which are settled for good or ill every night all over the world in similar fashion.

It is a putrid condition in the plague spots of the earth, and every man should make it his creed to help to restrain or stamp out, as he would any deadly disease, the vultures who thrive on it. And when the young men—for with them lies the remedy—who are too lackadaisical to bother, realise that the best men of the country are banding together for this very purpose, it behoves them to join the ranks, as every British man, who is a man, is doing, either actually or in spirit.

When San departed with the Lady Sybil, Wu Ling turned back to the pile of papers before him. So far as any outward signs were concerned, he showed no trace of being affected by the sentence he had just passed. Nor was he.

Prince Wu Ling was a man with just one purpose in life, and he was all the more dangerous to humanity because he was honest in that purpose, and, according to his rights, honourable in his methods.

That these did not coincide with the Anglo-Saxon idea of how things should be done is no reason why Wu Ling should be condemned, and on that very point had Sexton Blake shown the deep insight into human nature, and the complicated motives governing its actions, which he possessed.

That purpose was one which was a creed with Wu Ling. Descendant of a dynasty which could trace its history back to a time when the Anglo-Saxon race was unheard of, bred in the mystic lore of generations of ancient scholars, steeped in the pure philosophy of Confucius, and with an inborn reverence for Taoism, he felt to the uttermost depths of his nature that the Celestial race and no other was the race destined to be the rulers of the earth. To him the Anglo-Saxons were as flies of yesterday. In his heart he looked upon them as an accident of civilisation and the thieves of credit; thieves, because they made use of inventions ancient for centuries in China, and presented them to a credulous world as children of their own intelligence.

The utter indifference to human suffering and the apparent savagery of the Celestial caused the Anglo-Saxon to shudder with horror. To Wu Ling, the very sensitiveness which caused them to shudder was the token of an effeminate nature. He was the product of a school which believed in drastic measures where punishment was necessary, and would never have countenanced the more humane—to him the more effeminate—notions of the Anglo-Saxon.

It was his one dream to sow in their midst the seeds of discontent and terror, to play off one against the other, to pit white against white, and from the sowing to reap a crop of victory for his own kind; to feel the heel of the East on the West, to carve a path of saffron through a field of white, to raise on high Confucius, Buddha, and Taoism. That was his hope, his aim, and his ambition.

As a knock came at the door Wu Ling raised his eyes. As he thought, it was San, but, contrary to his expectations, his faithful lieutenant had not come to resume the work upon which they had been occupied. Instead, he stood just within the door, and bowing low, said:

"Excellency, the pig Looey Sing has arrived. He sends his unworthy homage to you, and begs your Excellency will grant him audience. He brings with him the man and girl of whom he spoke in his telegram, and also an old woman who looks after the girl."

"Is the girl conscious?" asked Wu Ling curtly.

"Yes, Excellency. The dog Looey Sing tells me he stopped the drug yesterday."

"Then I will grant audience. Let them all be brought before me."

San again bowed and departed. In a few minutes he returned. Behind him came Looey Sing, and following him Yvonne, leaning on the arm of an old woman, with Rymer bringing up the rear.

Wu Ling had turned his attention back to the papers before him, and probably it was because his head was bent over them that at first Rymer failed to recognise him.

Had he done so it is certain that his ideas of getting possession of the reward offered for the Lady Sybil, as well as his intentions regarding Yvonne, would have been thrust aside in one mad dash for safety, for Dr. Huxton Rymer and Prince Wu Ling had scores of old standing to settle.

Not recognising the prince, he followed the others across the room until they all stood before the desk. Then Wu Ling looked up. In one all-seeing glance his eyes swept the quartette before him until they came to rest on Rymer. Without the flicker of an eyelash he said curtly:

"San, lock the door. Put the key in your pocket."

With a surprising agility for one of his bulk, San obeyed, and Rymer, who had uttered one startled gasp of recognition, controlled his features, realising that if ever in his life, bluff and nerve were to serve him now was the time.

When San had returned to the side of his master Wu Ling turned to Looey Sing.

"You tell me of failure, Looey Sing," he said slowly. "Is that what I ask of you?"

The Celestial spread out his hands.

"Excellency, I have served faithfully. By day I have planned, by night I have worked. It is not the fault of Looey Sing. The man Blake left from Cardiff. He never reached Looey Sing. Had he done so I would have killed him. Instead, I risked all to go to the succour of the cargo. Those I bring with me I saved. Anything more was impossible, Excellency."

"Blake, Blake, always the man Blake!" mused Wu Ling, never taking his eyes off Looey Sing's face. But had he done so he would have seen the half-closed eyes of the girl with the glorious bronze-gold hair light up suddenly as the name left his lips.

"You speak the truth, Looey Sing," went on Wu Ling. "You have done well. I have indeed no blame for you. The fault lies with Sam Loo, a fault for which he shall pay dearly. Go now! I have things for you to do, and will talk with you to-morrow."

"Your unworthy servant is grateful, Excellency. Always will he serve you with his life."

With that Looey Sing departed, no doubt congratulating himself warmly, at the outcome of the dreaded interview with his chief.

At the same time it was only a sample of Wu Ling's justice, for the prince never punished unless punishment were deserved. When San had again locked the door and returned, Wu Ling ignored Yvonne for the time being, and turned to Rymer.

"Dr. Huxton Rymer," he said, gazing inscrutably at Rymer, "is it because you have my interests at heart that you come here to-night?"

For a moment Rymer was silent. Then he looked up.

"Wu Ling, I knew not that you were the head of the System when I joined it. At the same time I have worked for its interests, and at a time when all appeared to be lost I saved the most important part of the cargo at the risk of my life. She stands here before you."

"You lie!"

As Wu Ling uttered the words with deadly calm he leaned forward.

"Listen to me, Doctor Huxton Rymer! Do you think Wu Ling organises a System without having the means at hand to know everything which affects that system? Fool! Do you take me for a babe?

"Before me I have a report which tells me how you gained admittance to the crew of the Eastern Queen. Another report tells how you proclaimed yourself second mate in the private room at Sam Loo's. A third how you deserted the Eastern Queen in St. John, and joined the motor-boat Spitfire by saying the captain of the Eastern Queen had sent you. Again, you leave the schooner as a rat leaves a sinking ship, but you still continue on through the channel of the System. And now you stand and lie to me—Wu Ling!

"Do you forget that I know you to your very depths? Do you forget the time, when I dragged you out of an opium den, a weak, doddering imbecile, and put you on your feet? Do you forget your treachery when the American, John Strang, was in my power? And again, when in Ecuador you first sold the secret of a dead man to Andrades, the Spaniard, and in turn to sell us to the president? Bah! You child, to pit your wits against Wu Ling.

"For days have I sat here, waiting to see who the white man was who came with Looey Sing. I dared to hope that it was the man Blake walking into my arms. But, at least, he is no infant. You joined the System for some purpose of your own. It matters not now what it was, for it has failed. In any case, you are a traitor to the System, and by the rules of the Brotherhood all traitors are punished by death.

"But death will not be your reward, Dr. Huxton Rymer. From you will be exacted the payment for past treachery as well. And your punishment will be lifelong slavery in the rice fields of China, with the raw hide lash when you shirk. San, take him away!"

As San advanced to do his bidding, Rymer made a move as though to resist. The sight of a shining revolver in the hands of the latter, however, caused him to think better of it. He threw one strange look at Yvonne, who had listened with horror to the sentence, then with bowed head he turned and passed out.

As Yvonne turned back to Wu Ling, her eyes were swimming with tears, for though he had chosen the crooked path, Rymer had once been a gentleman. Moreover, he had expressed for Yvonne all the love his nature could feel, and it is hard for a woman to thoroughly hate the man who chooses her above all the world as the recipient of his love.

When Rymer was gone, Wu Ling looked at the old woman.

"Well, old hag, what have you to say?" he asked curtly. "You come from Sam Loo?" Mother Peters almost grovelled on the floor as she bobbed forward, and began a long-winded tale.

Wu Ling cut her short.

"Answer my questions!" he ordered. "Are you in charge of this girl?"

"Oh, yes, your Excellency!"

"To where is she bound?"

"To China, Excellency, to become the wife of the Governor of Hamai. I bear a letter to him."

"Give it to me!"

"Oh, yes, your Excellency!"

The cringing old woman drew out the letter and handed it to the prince, who, without looking at it, tore it to pieces and dropped it on the floor.

Then he turned to San.

"Take her out!" he ordered. "I will decide what is to be done with her!"

San obeyed, and was returning to take up his old position, when Wu Ling said:

"And, San, leave me for a bit."

With a murmured "Yes, Excellency," San passed out.

Then Wu Ling turned to Yvonne.

"And now, Mademoiselle Yvonne," he said softly, "we will talk."

"You--you--you!" whispered Yvonne, stumbling blindly towards Blake.

JUST about the time when Looey Sing, with Rymer and Yvonne, reached the end of their long drive, and entered the house near Kneeland Street which sheltered Wu Ling, the closely muffled figure of a Chinaman turned out of Harrison Avenue into Kneeland Street.

The hail and sleet were driving in off the bay with a terrific force, which sent all who could go into the warm protection of their homes.

The Chinaman who battled his way against it seemed utterly oblivious of the discomfort of it. In truth he was, for his thoughts were too absorbed in a certain problem to heed aught but the purpose on which he was bent.

Though he looked a Celestial in every particular, and though he had passed as one for many days, he was far from being one. Underneath that muffled exterior was the personality of Sexton Blake, and on this night he was on his way to put to the test the truth of information gained through many weary days.

When Blake astonished his companions on board the Fleur-de-Lys by deciding to give up the pursuit of those in the motor-boat and run for Boston, it had been no blind chance on which he was bent. Down in the solitude of his cabin he had marshalled before him all the facts which he possessed, and one by one had connected them up into a workable whole.

It seemed certain to him that, even did he succeed in tracing the trail taken by the occupants of the motor-boat, he would stand no chance of coming up with them before other developments had taken place, chief of which was the warning of the unshipped "cargo" which still waited in St. John.

Moreover, now that the cat was out of the bag, the smugglers along this particular underground route would abandon everything— at least, until the storm blew over. That being so, it meant that they would run for safety, and where more likely than to either the originating point of the System or the end of it.

As the originating point in Cardiff was known, and as the route through to the St. Croix River was also known, it left only the American side of which Blake and Kennedy were still ignorant.

It was certain that they would not double back, only to put their heads through the noose, but, instead, would scuttle for shelter at the other end. That might be Boston, New York, Chicago, or 'Frisco. Portland Blake discarded, for the reason that he considered it too small a city to be a final point in a system having such gigantic dimensions as the one upon which they had stumbled.

Boston being the nearest point, it was just possible they would make for there, and if so he might yet succeed in wresting success from apparent failure. It was at that point in his deductions that he rose and made his way to the bridge to give orders to make all speed for Boston.

A stop at Eastport on the way was necessary, in order that Kennedy might land. He was to go on to Boston by rail, and had arranged that, with a dozen Secret Service men, he would be on hand there night and day did Blake discover anything further. On that point Blake and Kennedy had their first difference of policy.

The American was all for gathering together a good-sized force, and making a clean sweep of the Chinese district in search for any Celestials without documents of authority proving they had a right to reside in the United States. Since half of the route had been discovered, it would not be difficult to discover the other half, once the ringleaders were in custody.

On that point Blake differed with him. He never for a moment forgot his promise to the Duchess of Carrisbrooke that if he succeeded in discovering the Lady Sybil all publicity would be rigorously suppressed. Now he had a further reason for desiring to work in secret, and that was Yvonne.

Did he adopt Kennedy's plan, and did a raid take place, every newspaper in the country would blazon forth the news on the following day. And if the two missing girls were discovered, then their names would come out. What a feast for the reporters to dwell upon! Mademoiselle Yvonne, the famous adventuress, and the Lady Sybil, daughter of the Duke and Duchess of Carrisbrooke, rescued from a Chinese den.

Blake squirmed when he thought of it. It was only by sticking doggedly to his point that he won out. He had pledged his word that, in return for Kennedy's guarantee of secrecy, he would not rest until he had placed in the hands of the American the exact route used from the time the "cargoes" crossed the American line.

From Eastport he sent a wire to the authorities in St, John, and had the satisfaction of receiving a reply saying the twenty-one

Celestials had been gathered in, and would be deported at once. Then he sent a cable to the chief of the Cardiff police, asking him to arrest Sam Loo.

Not until he got to Boston did he receive a reply to that. It said: "Sam Loo disappeared. It is stated he has returned to China."

And months later Blake discovered the Celestial had indeed gone to China, and had there paid the penalty which Wu Ling demanded.

At Boston Blake landed at night, and made his way towards Harrison Avenue.

No more was he disguised as the coolie Chen Foo, but now wore the richer robes of a Chinese merchant. Tinker, Pedro, and Graves had remained on board the yacht to await developments. If Blake had any success he was to let them know at once, and they, in turn, were to communicate with Kennedy. Then they would act.

From the moment the duchess had been startled by the sketch of Wu Ling, which stood on his desk, Blake had felt that in some way the prince was behind the whole system into which he had been so suddenly plunged.

If that were so, it was just possible that his search might eventually take him clear through to China, and if Wu Ling did chance to be at the head of it, Blake was inclined to hope it would, for not until he had tracked the nefarious business to the fountain head would he rest content.

Thus far had his deductions gone, when he made his way into the Chinese quarter of Boston for the first time. Five long days and nights did Blake spend there, and only the perfection of his disguise ever got him through with his life.

On the very first night he had sought lodgings behind a gambling-room, and had given out that he had come through by way of Mexico. As he knew the code greeting of the Brotherhood of the Yellow Beetle, it was not long before he was admitted freely to every place in the district.

Day and night he toiled, asking a careless question here, listening closely there. When alone in his room, he would jot down the information gained, and what an array of names he had gathered. Sixty-eight in all there were, every one of which was the name of a Celestial without the papers of residence which he should have possessed. Only on the fifth day did he discover that a suppressed air of excitement, which hung over the quarter, was due to the expected arrival of no less a personage than Wu Ling himself, who was coming through, incognito, to hold a conference of the Eastern section of the Brotherhood. A little judicious questioning on Blake's part, revealed the place where Wu Ling was to stay.

That afternoon he sent a long code message to the yacht, and when the evening was well advanced, he bundled up, and went out into the storm. He was on his way to play the final trick in the game, and none knew better than Blake the calibre of the opponent against whom he was to be pitted.

Anticipating every unexpected thing which was liable to occur, even Blake did not guess that, at that very moment, Yvonne was standing alone before Wu Ling.

It had been no small surprise to her to discover that Wu Ling had recognised her so promptly, for though, during her period of unconsciousness, any marks of disguise had been practically erased, her very pallor seemed to her to change her appearance to a wonderful extent.

She had possessed little notion that her daring plan was to lead her into the clutches of Wu Ling, and though his words still rang in her ears, she was silent, thinking desperately what line to take. She realised thoroughly that, unless succour reached her from some source within a very short time, she would be forced to drink to the dregs the bitter cup of suffering.

Wu Ling sat waiting patiently for her to speak, watching her as a cat does a mouse. Now that he had her in his hands he had no intention of hastening matters.

A low knock at the door at that moment brought a crease of irritation to his brow, and a sigh of relief from Yvonne. It meant that, at least, she would gain a few minutes respite, and could better decide what course to pursue.

Wu Ling curtly cried "Enter!" and, as the door opened, San appeared, bowing apologetically.

"Excellency," he said, "your unworthy servant prays your forgiveness, but one is below who insists upon seeing your Excellency."

"Who is it?" asked Wu Ling.

"He gives no name, Excellency, but bade me by the oath of the Brotherhood to seek you at once and crave from you an immediate interview. The unspeakable dog says his unworthy business is of an urgent nature, Excellency!"

"Since he is of the Brotherhood, and seeks by the oath, I can but see him," replied Wu Ling slowly. "Take this girl away, San. I will talk with her when he is gone. Send him up!"

San bowed, and taking Yvonne by the arm, disappeared through the door. Less than five minutes later, it opened to admit the muffled figure of a Celestial, from whose coat the melting snow still dripped.

He closed the door, and coolly locked it; then he tossed aside his coat, and bowed low to Wu Ling.

"Prince Wu Ling, it was somewhat of a surprise to know you were in Boston; but since you are here, I have sought you. We have business to discuss."

For the space of a full minute Wu Ling regarded the man who had dared to enter and speak in such terms to the autocratic head of the Brotherhood of the Yellow Beetle.

At the end of that time, his lids dropped with a barely perceptible motion, and one slim, sensitive yellow hand stretched out and rested palm down on the table.

"So," he said softly, "it is you, Sexton Blake. At last you have come!"

Blake bowed ironically.

"As you see, Wu Ling. I have come, but not as you hope."

"You talk bravely, my friend," rejoined the prince. "Do you think, then, you can walk into the lair of the tiger and escape unscathed?"

"Not only do I think so," responded Blake, stepping forward a pace, "but Wu Ling, I know so. Moreover, when I leave the lair of the tiger, I shall leave not only unscathed, but with that which I have come to get!"

"Indeed! Do you think, Sexton Blake, that Prince Wu Ling is the man to court defeat in a meeting for which he has been longing? Is the past nothing to me? Is it only to forget that under certain circumstances I was compelled to yield to you? Is it for nothing that I learn how you befooled Sam Loo in Cardiff, and betrayed to the authorities the system I took months to organise? Is Wu Ling the man to forget these things? No; a thousand times no, Sexton Blake!

"You and I have been ranged on opposite sides ever since the man Halliday escaped from China with the secret of the Yellow Beetle. Destiny, which up to now has been against me, has at last placed you in my hands. It has, indeed, been kind to me this night. From the wreckage of the System have come many whom I sought. The exposure was worth it. And now, if you have anything to say, say it, for soon you go to meet the fate in store for you."

"You talk with confidence, Wu Ling," replied Blake coldly. "It is not like you to boast without reason, and yet on this occasion you do so. Not yet has the time come when I go to meet what fate you choose to give me. Instead, I come tonight to make demands—demands which you will grant. Even as you sit there so confidently, Prince Wu Ling, you are at my mercy. And now I will tell you why I have come."

"I have told you to speak."

"I have come to demand from you the person of the Lady Sybil Druce, daughter of the Duke and Duchess of Carrisbrooke, who has fallen into your power."

"Might I ask what makes you so positive?"

"Certainly. The fact that Wu Ling and Dr. Li-Fuang are one and the same is the reason. Secondly, I demand the person of the young woman who reached Boston this week. She was the last portion of cargo through the underground system, so no mistake will be made as to whom I mean. Thirdly, I demand the peaceful surrender of the following Celestials, at present residing in this district, and not possessing papers of residence!"

As he spoke, Blake drew out a long sheet of paper, and began reading out the list of names he had copied during the past few days. When he had finished, he looked up.

"That, Wu Ling, is what I demand!"

"Since you make your demands so boldly, perhaps you will enlighten me as to how you expect to enforce them."

"Certainly. My cards will all be laid on the table, Wu Ling. In the first place, I may say that at this very moment the place is surrounded by a large force of Secret Service men under Mr. Kennedy, of whom you will have heard. If I am in here longer than a certain period of time, they will at once raid the premises. In his possession is a sealed envelope containing a list of the sixty-eight men I have named.

"If I fail, he is to open it, and a clean sweep of the district will follow. Not only will those sixty-eight be captured, but every man who possesses no residence papers. Moreover, many of those who are legally entitled to reside here will be deported for conspiracy. I do not think for a moment that such a raid will touch the person of Prince Wu Ling, for you will, of course, be provided with diplomatic papers making you immune from the law of the land. Great publicity will follow, however, and I do not think, Wu Ling, that such a thing will fit in with your plans.

"I have also taken the precaution to send to my assistant a sealed envelope to pass on to the Duke of Carrisbrooke, should anything happen to me while I am in here. I leave you to judge what action will be taken by England if they discover you have abducted the daughter of a man who ranks as high as does the duke, and who went to your country on a special mission.

"In order to make my demands definite, Wu Ling, I have been compelled to consider many things. The demand for the sixty-eight men whose names I have given you is for Kennedy. This I was compelled to promise him in order to prevent him from raiding the district without delay and making a clean sweep. Since it was through my efforts that your System was broken up and your cargo captured, he was compelled to accept my terms, as you will have to do.

"My reason is simple. I wish no publicity any more than do you. Neither your country nor mine can tolerate a diplomatic complication of such a description at the present time. You know that is a fact. What duty I owed to the United States I have performed. It is now for me to bring to a completion the rest of my purpose, and for that reason I have made the foregoing demands and conditions. There is one more demand which I make."

"It is?"

"A description of the route by which your cargoes were brought to Boston after crossing the line between the United States and Canada. And in regard to the two prisoners I have demanded, Wu Ling, an essential condition is that they be unharmed. Now your answer."

"Your demands are far from modest, Sexton Blake," answered Wu Ling slowly. "To-night there have come into my hands many whom I sought, I swore that the vengeance of the Brotherhood should be dealt out to each—you included. Is it now for me to alter my decision, and again yield to you? No."

"Listen, Wu Ling," said Blake curtly. "It is not a case of what you wish. It is a case in which you are helpless. You have much more to lose than you have to gain by refusing my demands. If that were not so, should I be fool enough to walk in here without a weapon of any description?

"In the past we have been opposed on many occasions. You know me well enough to be aware that I never strike unless I know where my blow will fall. The day must come when these struggles between us must end. It is not the law of Nature that they should continue."

"And for that day I pray," interrupted Wu Ling sombrely. "You are cunning with the cunning of the East, Sexton Blake. It is true that greater things are at stake than revenge on those whom I hold. The demands you make must be granted in order that other matters may be saved."

As Wu Ling made his dignified avowal of defeat, something inside Blake suddenly relaxed, and for the first time he realised the cold beads were standing out on his forehead. Simple though the words were, he knew what a depth of meaning they held, and what a crashing blow it must be to Wu Ling to see victory snatched from his very grasp. And yet, true to his nature, the Celestial betrayed not the slightest sign of the tumult raging inside him.

Blake took another step forward, and spoke very slowly:

"In that case, Wu Ling, I will ask you a favour."

"What is it?"

"That you have brought here at once the young woman who last arrived."

"You mean Mademoiselle Yvonne?"

"Then you know?" asked Blake quickly.

For the first time a smile broke across Wu Ling's features.

"Am I an infant?" he said curtly. "It shall be as you wish. Unlock the door. I will ring."

Blake turned to the door with an extraordinary feeling tugging at his heart. His pride would not permit him to ask if Yvonne were safe and well, but an unaccustomed frenzy of impatience filled him as he waited for Wu Ling's ring to be answered. And, throbbing in his brain, was the thought that he and he alone had saved her.

San answered the ring, and Wu Ling curtly bade him to bring Yvonne.

A moment later she came, looking strangely like a tired child, with the pallor of her face throwing into relief the big deep-blue eyes and the tangled bronze hair falling in distracting masses over the drooping neck. Little did she dream that she was coming to Blake. To her it was but a summons to hear what Wu Ling had not had time to say.

As she entered she glanced dully at Blake, who stood facing her, his eyes no longer those of the Chinese merchant, but keen and wide as usual, and yet filled with a wonderful tenderness.

Slowly the tremendous truth beat its way into Yvonne's mind. Her eyes grew misty, and her lips trembled as she drew in her breath sharply. Every feature of the man she loved with all her nature stood out clear and white, stripped of its disguise. A wayward hand brushed across her eyes, but the mist of happiness could only yield to the joy of realisation.

Blake took a step towards her, and as his movement told her he was no chimera of a distraught mind, but a glorious, living reality, she stumbled, blindly towards him, her arms outstretched, and he caught her just as she gave a low moan and collapsed.

Blake held her very tenderly, and pushed the heavy hair back from her head. He could feel her heart beating wildly with the throbbing relief of the bird who has reached the shelter of the nest before the hawk could strike.

She had not fainted, for she stirred slightly, and opened her eyes.

"You—you—you," she whispered, feeding her eyes on his, the while her hand beat aimlessly against his shoulder.

Blake bent his head until his lips were very close to her ear. The sweet perfume of her hair assailed him, and its soft masses brushed his eyes. For a moment he closed his lids, then he whispered:

"It is all right now, little girl. You are safe, and no harm shall come to you."

Yvonne's white arm crept up until it rested against his cheek, then her soft fingers fluttered lightly over his face.

"You; oh, it is you!" she whispered again. "I knew you would come."

Blake lifted his head, and, with his arm supporting her, led her gently across to a chair.

"We shall leave soon," he said, smiling. "There are one or two things yet to be attended to."

He turned to speak to Wu Ling, but discovered, with surprise, that he was no longer sitting at the table. As he turned back the door again opened, and the prince entered, followed by the Lady Sybil, who gazed in surprise at Yvonne.

How Wu Ling had departed so quickly Blake didn't know, but a panel in the wall near the table would have explained the mystery had he investigated it.

When the prince had once more taken his seat he turned to the Lady Sybil.

"When you were in here before," he said curtly, "I told you what I desired of you. Since then conditions have changed. You are free to go."

As the girl stared stupidly, Blake stepped forward, and in a few quiet words explained who he was. She listened in stupefaction at the unexpected news, and when he saw she was on the point of breaking down, Blake motioned to Yvonne. In her happiness, Yvonne yielded to the other all the sweet consolation of her nature, and as she led the Lady Sybil aside, Blake said, with a fleeting smile:

"I told you on Christmas Eve, I should need you to look after her."

And Yvonne flashed back softly:

"And I told you I should always be ready to do so."

Then Blake approached the table, and sat down beside Wu Ling.

"Now, prince," he said quietly, "if you will kindly give me the route of the System, we will make arrangements for the handing over of the sixty-eight men to Kennedy."

For fully a quarter of an hour Blake was bent in concentrated attention while Wu Ling sketched out on a map a detailed outline of the way the cargoes were brought after leaving the Canadian side. When the prince had finished Blake folded up the map and thrust it in his pocket.

As he rose a soft swish sounded behind him, and he felt a small hand on his arm. Turning, he gazed up into Yvonne's eyes.

"What is it?" he asked, with a smile.

"It is Rymer," she whispered. "He has been condemned to lifelong slavery in the rice-fields. Won't you save him?"

"It is strange to hear you pleading for Rymer," answered Blake, with a touch of coldness in his tones.

"Oh, please do not misunderstand me!" she pleaded hurriedly. "He is a white man, and, no matter what he has done to you and me, it would be awful to let him go into that living hell."

"I will see what I can do," said Blake thoughtfully, turning back to Wu Ling.

The prince showed no signs as to whether or not he had heard Yvonne's request. He still sat as inscrutable as ever. Blake regarded him for a moment, then he spoke.

"Prince Wu Ling," he said slowly, "when I came here to-night I made certain demands and laid down certain conditions, to which you agreed."

"That is right," responded the other calmly.

"That being so, I can make no fresh demands," went on Blake. "And yet, Wu Ling, I would ask a favour."

"I listen."

"It is that you hand over to me the man Rymer."

"It is impossible," answered Wu Ling curtly. "Though we are on opposite sides, and though your race and mine must one day crash together in a final struggle, I have for you the love of a brother, Sexton Blake, though when I can sweep you from my path I shall do so. If you asked me anything material I would gladly give it to you as the recognition of man to man. And always you know that if you will join us, the East will receive you and place you second only to Wu Ling. But what you ask to-night I cannot grant. I have waited long to got my hands on the traitor Rymer, and now that I have him I shall not let him go."

Blake's eyes dropped in thought as Wu Ling finished. He realised the truth and justice of the reply from Wu Ling's point of view, but, if he could, he would grant Yvonne's plea.

Ever so slowly his hand went beneath his jacket, and emerged a moment later bearing a chamois bag containing something round. He paid no heed to Yvonne's smothered exclamation as she saw what it was, but began methodically to undo the string which held it together.

A moment later the light gleamed on an exquisite jade sphere as it slipped into his hand, and he held it out to Wu Ling.

"Will you give me Rymer for this?" he said softly. "You, Wu Ling, are the representative of the ancient Ming Dynasty. It is unnecessary to tell you what it is which I hold in my hand."

Not even Wu Ling's inborn capacity of repression could withstand the shock as his eyes rested on the Sacred Sphere which for two hundred and fifty years had been lost. His eyes closed as a sharp pain assailed him, and his long fingers curled up in a paroxysm of emotion.

Blake sat motionless, waiting.

Finally the prince got slowly to his feet and held out his hand,

"How you came to possess the Sacred Sphere of the Son of Heaven I do not ask," he said in a voice utterly unlike his own. "You ask me will I give you the man Rymer for it? I would give a thousand such dogs! I would give life, honour, wealth! I would give a kingdom!"

"Then take it, Wu Ling," said Blake quietly. "It is yours."

Slowly the hand of the prince stretched out until his fingers hovered over the sacred symbol of his line. So tense was the silence that Blake could hear the two girls breathing in suspense. Probably never in the annals of history had such a priceless treasure returned to its own in a more dramatic manner. In that moment Blake confessed to himself that Wu Ling was the true prince and worthy representative of the Ming Dynasty.

As Wu Ling's fingers closed on the sphere, and found it no mad dream but a reality, a shudder went through him, and he sank back into his chair.

Blake rose at once.

"If you will give orders to one of your men, Wu Ling, I shall be going."

The prince touched a bell, and as San appeared he said:

"Conduct Mr. Blake outside. Hand over to him the man Rymer and the men whose names he will give you. If he desires anything else give it to him."

The faithful San gazed stupidly at his master, wondering what had come over him; but at a gesture from the prince he turned and started out. As the others followed, Blake and Yvonne looked back.

There sat Wu Ling, with the sphere before him. In his hand was the golden god Mo which he always carried before him. His eyes were closed. He was praying.

"I am glad now you gave it to him," whispered Yvonne, laying her fingers on Blake's arm.

"And I," he said, as he slipped his hand over hers.

And so they went out together, leaving the prince to his golden god, his prayers, and the Sacred Sphere.

•   •   •   •   •

When Rymer came stumbling out of the room where he had been confined, not knowing what Fate held in store for him, Blake stepped forward and looked him in the eyes.

"Rymer," he said curtly, "you were condemned to slavery in the rice-fields of China. Knowing nothing of it, I would have done nothing to save you from it. Mademoiselle Yvonne, however, has seen fit to plead for you, and her plea has been granted. You belong to her, and what she says shall be done."

Then he turned, to Yvonne.

"Mademoiselle," he said, "what is your wish?"

Yvonne looked up at Rymer.

"You deserve little from me, Dr. Rymer," she said, "and if we meet again on an equal footing I shall exact payment for every moment of suffering you have caused me. At the same time, I do not wish to strike you when you are helpless. My desire is that you go, and I hope I shall never see you again!"

Rymer listened with bowed head to Yvonne's words. All the decency in the man's nature had risen to suffer the shame of his position. When he had finished he lifted his head as though to speak; then he thought better of it, and turning, passed slowly out of the room.

Ten minutes later Yvonne and the Lady Sybil had been handed over to the care of Graves and Alec, who lost no time in getting them to the yacht. Tinker remained with Blake, and the two were soon busy checking over the list of names as San produced the men Blake called for and handed them over into the custody of Kennedy and his deputies.

How Blake had managed it the latter couldn't begin to guess, but when the list finished, Blake drew out the map and gave it to the American. Kennedy held out his hand.

"You have made it possible for me to make the biggest scoop on record, Blake," he said huskily. "I shall never forget this as long as I live!"

Blake gripped his hand warmly.

"And secrecy is the watchword," he said, with a smile.

"I pledge you my word none but my chief shall know the true facts," replied Kennedy.

Then, after shaking hands with Tinker, he went off with his men, and Blake, with a look of deep weariness in his eyes, started with Tinker for the yacht.

Whether he was thinking of Yvonne or whether he was thinking of Wu Ling it is hard to say, nor would any but himself know the reason of any weariness of soul which assailed him.

Such was the man Sexton Blake.

•   •   •   •   •

It may seem strange to think of Christmas festivities being held after that great day is past, but so it was on board the yacht Fleur-de-Lys as she steamed on her way from Boston to London.

A cable had been sent telling the duke and duchess of Blake's success, and under Yvonne's care the Lady Sybil had entirely recovered. Most of the members of that party had passed through too much not to feel the relief.

It was on the first night out that the Christmas banquet was held. Captain Vaughan was at one end of the table, with the Lady Sybil on his right. Yvonne was at the other end, with Blake beside her. Tinker was on Yvonne's left, and across from him was Graves.

For once in his life Blake blushed as Graves gave a rousing toast to the man who had brought to others the happiness they felt that night, and for the moment his weariness passed as Yvonne lifted her glass and gazed at him ever so softly with a look of sweet challenge in her misty eyes.

THE END.
[68000 WORDS]

THE END.

www.ingramcontent.com/pod-product-compliance
Lightning Source LLC
Chambersburg PA
CBHW020441180626
46812CB00003B/1348